"Don't Come Any Closer!

I mean it, Yale. I don't want you touching me. Not ever!"

"But I *am* going to touch you," he promised with silky menace. "Often, and in the most delightful places. You belong to me now, temper and all. As I said, I'm satisfied with the transaction and I'll make sure you are, too. . . ."

Dara's eyes blazed as she realized she was trapped. "You really can't get it through that thick head of yours that I didn't go with you in order to get your account, can you? Well, I didn't! I don't want your account! I never cared one way or the other about it!"

"Too bad, because you're stuck with it," he gritted, his fingers curling over her bare shoulders. "And believe me, I'll make you pay for every dollar you lose!"

STEPHANIE JAMES

readily admits that the chief influence on her writing is her "lifelong addiction to romantic daydreaming." She has spent the last nine years living and working with her engineer husband in a wide variety of places, including the Caribbean, the Southeast and the Pacific Northwest. Ms. James currently resides in California.

Dear Reader:

SILHOUETTE DESIRE is an exciting new line of contemporary romances from Silhouette Books. During the past year, many Silhouette readers have written in telling us what other types of stories they'd like to read from Silhouette, and we've kept these comments and suggestions in mind in developing SILHOUETTE DESIRE.

DESIREs feature all of the elements you like to see in a romance, plus a more sensual, provocative story. So if you want to experience all the excitement, passion and joy of falling in love, then SILHOUETTE DESIRE is for you.

I hope you enjoy this book and all the wonderful stories to come from SILHOUETTE DESIRE. I'd appreciate any thoughts you'd like to share with us on new SILHOUETTE DESIRE, and I invite you to write to us at the address below:

Karen Solem
Editor-in-Chief
Silhouette Books
P.O. Box 769
New York, N.Y. 10019

STEPHANIE JAMES
Reckless Passion

Silhouette Desire

Published by Silhouette Books New York

America's Publisher of Contemporary Romance

SILHOUETTE BOOKS, a Simon & Schuster Division of
GULF & WESTERN CORPORATION
1230 Avenue of the Americas, New York, N.Y. 10020

ISBN: 0-671-44806-4

First Silhouette Books printing December, 1982

10 9 8 7 6 5 4 3 2 1

For my husband Frank—
with all my love and the futile hope that someday he will learn not to flinch at the total of a writer's monthly phone bill.

1

"Exactly how far can I expect the seduction to go?" Yale Ransom inquired interestedly in his pleasant Southern drawl.

Dara Bancroft froze momentarily in the act of letting him assist her into the chic suede and leather coat. Some of the inexplicable warmth she had been experiencing all evening faded.

"Seduction?" she repeated carefully, her gently rounded chin lifting in a wary gesture. "I don't know what you're talking about. If that's the reason you think I've agreed to leave the party with you . . ."

"Don't take offense, honey," he soothed at once, his strong hands sliding the coat into place on her shoulders. The hands didn't look at all like an accountant's hands, Dara realized. Poor man. He tried so hard, but little things kept giving him away.

"I'm more than willing to be seduced," he went on easily, holding the door open and ushering her out into the chilly spring night. "After all, I'm in the market for a stockbroker, and your manager has made it clear Edison, Stanford and Zane would like my account."

"Mr. Ransom," Dara began firmly, hesitating on the top step as he took her arm, "I'm not sure how business is transacted down in Los Angeles, but here in Oregon we don't do things that way!"

"What a shame," he murmured, politely regretful. "And it can be such a pleasure, too."

Dara's expressive mouth curved into a knowing smile. "Careful, Yale. Your Southern-gentleman facade is slipping."

He grimaced wryly. "Already? And I try so hard."

"I know you do." Dara chuckled, yielding to the pressure of his hand and descending the steps toward a gray Alfa Romeo which waited on the street in front of the house. "But you don't have to pretend around me, Yale."

He shot her a slanting, hazel-eyed look as they walked toward the car, the dark horn rims of his glasses not concealing the speculative expression in his gaze. "You know me so well? After only a couple of hours?"

"We stockbrokers are trained to analyze situations quickly," Dara responded with a satisfied smile.

"And in that short span of time you've decided I'm not the Southern-gentleman type, is that it?" he invited, settling her into the car.

"Oh, you've done a good job with the role and you've tried to create a proper, conservative accountant's image, but . . ."

"But?" he prompted, sliding onto the seat beside her and closing his door. It made that nice, solid sound that expensive car doors make.

"But I think you've been a lot of things in your life besides an accountant with a Southern accent!" she told him recklessly, unable to stifle the pleasant, heady rush which was swirling through her veins.

The sensation had taken her by storm almost two hours ago when she'd held out her hand for the conventional introduction her manager was making. Dara had smiled up into a pair of intelligent, interested hazel eyes and wondered what sort of expression she would see behind the lenses of his glasses when that deliberately neutral look was banished.

And then Yale Ransom had smiled back, a wide, faintly dangerous grin that must have been a reaction to her own challenging gray-green gaze. The flash from a gold-capped tooth added an astonishingly sharklike touch to Yale's raffish expression, and the strength of his grip on her hand told Dara a great deal more about the stranger.

He hadn't stayed a stranger for long. Almost instantly they had become paired off, with, Dara knew, the blessings of her manager, who was giving the party. But Dara didn't care if she was being used to attract Yale Ransom's account. She had other, more personal interests in the matter.

There was something about this man, she thought a little dazedly as Yale pulled away from the curb and drove down the quiet neighborhood streets of Eugene, Oregon. Something which pulled at her senses. Something had clicked between them.

On the surface, there was no logical explanation for her having singled him out of a roomful of people. He was exactly what he purported to be. Almost too much so, she decided, mentally casting about for what set him apart.

Perhaps that was the answer. Yale Ransom took great pains to conform to the image that was expected of him. The dark, amber honey of his hair was trimmed in a close, conservative style that went perfectly with the equally conservative horn-rimmed glasses. Folks here in the Willamette Valley of Oregon weren't inclined to be trendy, but even in this conservative atmosphere Yale

11

Ransom's dark jacket, slacks and subdued tie could be considered sober attire.

The crisp white of his shirt collar contrasted with the deep tan of a ruggedly carved face that had crinkles at the eyes and a certain implacability around the mouth. He must have been around thirty-seven or thirty-eight, Dara thought fleetingly, eyeing his firm profile as they drove. The years showed.

Yes, everything about him said conservative, quiet, studied, trustworthy, professional, she thought in amusement. Even the faint Southern accent added a nice touch of the old-fashioned gentleman. She wondered if the drawl was a calculated addition to the overall image. Perhaps it was designed to give the impression of a man who still held such virtues as honor in high esteem.

Because if this man had been raised amid magnolia blossoms, genteel poverty or moneyed aristocracy, Dara would cheerfully eat her leather and suede coat.

The hardness about this man belied the image of quiet gentleman. It was everywhere in him, from the harshly carved features of a face that had never been handsome to the six feet of smoothly muscled, hard male body. The conservative jacket and slacks did not hide the lean power underneath, at least not from Dara's eyes. And the lenses of his glasses couldn't conceal the perceptive, yet withdrawn expression of Yale's hazel gaze.

Given her own analysis, Dara told herself she ought to be wary of the man. He wasn't her type, and at the age of thirty, she thought she ought to know exactly what sort of man wasn't her type! But when he'd smiled at her, that exciting, daring grin with the flash of buccaneering gold, his carefully contrived image had shattered.

After that, everything about him had intrigued her. The strong hands, the hazel eyes, the contrast between the look he was trying to project and what she felt was the real man—it all added up to a fascinating puzzle.

"Where are we going?" she asked presently, not overly concerned. They were driving past the two-hundred-and-fifty-acre campus of the University of Oregon located in the eastern part of town.

"Does it matter?" Yale asked politely, his attention on his driving.

"Yes, I think so," Dara told him, considering the issue with a delicate frown. "I'm not ready to go home with you now, Yale."

"I see," he murmured after a moment, slowing the car and guiding it to a halt at the curb. With an efficient, decisive movement he switched off the engine and turned to look at her in the pale light of an overhead streetlamp.

"Implying that you will be ready to go home with me later?" he went on casually, hazel eyes flickering over her figure.

Dara's smile was slow and gently condescending. "I keep telling you, Yale, we don't do things that quickly here in Eugene. I left the party with you because you suggested we might go to a nightclub and have a drink and a few dances. Don't tell me you don't dance," she added, eyes glinting in the dim light. "Anyone who's worked on the image as much as you have must have learned to dance somewhere along the line!"

His answering smile spoke volumes. "I can manage. Where would you like to go? As you keep reminding me, I'm new here in town. I don't know all the in places yet." He waited, deliberately putting the responsibility on her.

"There aren't that many of them," Dara said dryly. "Eugene is only a town of about a hundred thousand. But we get along. Let me see . . ." Idly she chewed a full lower lip and thought about it for a moment. Yale didn't move, his eyes centered on her face. There was a quiet patience about him that amused her. He was so sure he knew how the evening was going to end.

13

It wouldn't wind up as he assumed it would, of course, she told herself briskly. Dara didn't attempt to deny the strange attraction he held for her, but she knew herself well enough to know she could handle her own emotions.

Until she had unraveled the puzzle that was Yale Ransom, she would be reasonably cautious. What did he think of her? Dara wondered in the back of her mind. He had seemed willing enough to accept the pairing off which had occurred. Of course, he *was* new in town and probably hadn't met a lot of women yet, she assured herself.

She wondered vaguely how she looked to him after his previous two years spent in Los Angeles. Dara was an honest individual. She knew there was a softness about her which more than one male had assumed extended to her brain as well as her body.

She couldn't really blame a man for thinking that, Dara had decided several years earlier. The gently rounded outlines of her five-foot-four-inch body could most graciously be described as full-figured. She was not fat, she assured herself several times a week, but there was no denying the fullness of her high, curving breasts or the rounded outline of her hips.

Her eyes echoed the softness of her body. Wide, faintly slanting and gray-green in color, they were full of laughter and an abiding interest in life. A short nose which turned up slightly at the tip, a mouth designed for smiling and an unaggressive, rounded chin gave her an impish, amused look which somehow managed to conceal the lack of any real beauty.

The burnt russet of her hair was styled in a sleek, center-parted bell which curved over her ears and ended even with the line of her jaw. The entire combination could be termed reasonably attractive, if a little misleading in that it hid a finely honed willpower, but it would never be described as sophisticated, Dara knew. Or even sweetly beautiful. So what did Yale Ransom really think of her? Had he been joking earlier when he'd implied a willingness to be seduced in exchange for his securities account?

"If you can't make up your mind," Yale interrupted softly, "perhaps we ought to continue on to my house. We can enjoy a glass of brandy while you decide where you want to go dancing."

He moved slightly, shifting one large hand on the steering wheel. The small action drew Dara's attention and her eyes focused for a split second on the muscular wrist which extended, she felt certain, from a sinewy forearm. She met his eyes again and he smiled, unwisely revealing the gold tooth which gave him such a feral look. With a suddenness that was typical of her, Dara made up her mind.

"That's all right," she said kindly. "But I've managed to make a decision. Turn left up there at the corner. I'll direct you."

Yale hesitated, tilting his head consideringly. Then, with a shrug, he started the engine again and followed her instructions.

With a concealed grin, Dara guided him through town to an elegantly rustic restaurant and nightclub. The parking lot was full and the Alfa Romeo had to be left on the street.

"You're sure this is where you want to spend the evening?" Yale asked warily as he assisted Dara out of the car.

"It's the latest rage," she told him saucily, smoothing her coat as she stepped from the car. Dara lifted her collar against the night chill and it framed her mischievous smile as she looked up at her escort.

"We're, uh, not exactly dressed for it," Yale observed, glancing down at his own conservative clothes and then at her. Under the leather and suede coat, Dara was wearing a softly cut, long-sleeved dress of emerald green. It shaped the fullness of her curves with a touch of sophistication which had pleased her when she'd surveyed herself in the mirror earlier.

"I think," she told him politely, "that if you take off your tie and unbutton your jacket, we'll get by. They get all types in here."

"All types but the one they're trying to imitate," Yale remarked, his fingers rising hesitantly to the knot of his tie. He glanced again at the jazzy sign with the neon-lit picture of a sequin-studded cowboy. The latest in country-western music drifted out into the parking lot.

"Well, you wouldn't want the real thing here, would you?" Dara challenged laughingly. "Genuine truckers and cowboys tend to be a bit rough around the edges, I'm told. The ones in designer jeans are easier to handle."

"You think so?" Yale asked, deciding at last not to undo the tie. Apparently he felt more comfortable in it, Dara thought in smiling amusement.

"Don't chicken out on me," Dara warned. "I'll take care of you."

He glanced at her over his shoulder as he closed the car door again. The hazel eyes flashed for an instant behind the lenses of his glasses. "Will you?" he demanded interestedly, taking her arm.

"Oh, yes," she assured him breezily. "I know this isn't quite your usual style, but I think the experience will be good for you."

"Are you by any chance trying to tell me I'm a little too conservative for your tastes?" Yale took her arm in a firm grip.

"I think, perhaps, you're a little too conservative for your own tastes," Dara hazarded.

"I would have thought that, as a stockbroker, you'd appreciate my conventional qualities," he told her dryly.

16

"Well, you see, I haven't been a stockbroker very long," Dara explained lightly.

"Really? What did you do before you became one?" He sounded genuinely interested, she thought, smiling.

"Remind me to tell you someday."

At the entrance to the disco, which had recently converted to high-gloss country-western, Dara and Yale came to a halt. The crowd of trendy would-be cowboys and their dates filled the room completely. A smoky haze wafted toward the wood-beamed ceiling and through it a bejeweled country-western band could be seen energetically twanging their electric guitars.

"See? I told you. It's a very popular place," Dara pointed out unnecessarily, scanning the room for a vacant table. From the height of five feet four inches she didn't stand a chance of discovering a spot.

"Over there." Above the noise Yale managed to get her attention.

"See something?"

He nodded and made his way through the crowd. He had been right when he noted they probably weren't dressed for the occasion. The majority of the club's clientele was in designer jeans and pearl-buttoned shirts. Imitation Stetson hats were everywhere, as was imported beer.

"Marvelous going out with a strong male," Dara said in tones of mocking admiration as Yale forged a way to the table and commandeered it.

"We accountants have hidden talents," he told her, helping her off with the coat.

"How hidden?" she demanded immediately, gray-green eyes shining with warm laughter as he took the seat across from her. "That's what I'm trying to find out."

"Then you should have let me take you home instead of stopping off here," he retorted, looking up as a briefly clad cowgirl came to take their order. He requested two bottles of a distinctive English beer without bothering to check Dara's preference. She didn't mind. It was the proper thing to order in this atmosphere.

"Something tells me I shall learn more about you in this environment," Dara informed him blandly.

"You think I belong here?" Yale glanced around dubiously.

"Doesn't it remind you of L.A.?" she asked innocently.

"Nothing is like L.A.!" he declared flatly, a disgusted look crossing the hard features.

"You miss it?"

"Not in the least."

"I believe you said you lived there for two years," Dara noted. "Where were you before that?"

One amber brow climbed slightly as he folded his arms and leaned forward to rest them on the small table. "Am I going to be subjected to an inquisition?"

"I always like to interview my clients extensively before establishing a financial plan for them," Dara said smoothly, eyes glinting.

"As I said, you should have let me take you straight home." He smiled. "I could have given you a much clearer insight into my character."

"Who is supposed to be seducing whom?" Dara's laughing eyes hardened a fraction.

"You're right," Yale said, instantly apologetic. "I'm being much too aggressive, aren't I?"

"I'm afraid you're in for a disappointment," Dara said kindly, sitting back slightly as the English beer arrived. She watched him pay the cocktail waitress and then continued charmingly, "I don't seduce potential clients—physically, that is. I prefer the intellectual approach. Makes for a better long-term working relationship."

"The intellectual approach?" He looked skeptical as he poured the foaming beer into a tall glass. "You're going to wow me with your brilliant market strategy?"

18

"Something like that. After all, if I bring my taxes to you to prepare I'm going to want some assurance you can at least use a calculator."

"Meaning it wouldn't matter how good I am in bed?" he said wistfully, sipping his beer.

Dara gave him a haughty look, torn between laughter and the need to put him in his place. Already the polite, conservative image was slipping away. She had been right to force him gently out of his adopted element in an effort to discover what lay below the surface, but it suddenly occurred to her that what she uncovered might not be quite so manageable. At least in the guise of conservative accountant, Yale Ransom could be easily dealt with.

"Meaning you ought to have some interest in my ability as a stockbroker!"

"I'll find out soon enough, won't I?" he countered.

"You're going to give Edison, Stanford and Zane your account?" she pressed.

"Probably. This is a small town. It's not as if I had a great deal of choice," he said smoothly.

"True." She grinned wickedly.

"What remains to be seen is whether or not I get you for my personal broker."

"Surely you're not going to tell me that will depend on how agreeable I am tonight?" Dara said loftily, daring him to come right out and proposition her.

As she had expected, Yale backed down from a direct confrontation on the subject. Something flickered and was gone in the hazel eyes, and she nodded to herself, satisfied.

"I didn't think so," she said sweetly. "Now, are you going to dance with me?"

"I already feel rather out of place just sitting here," he complained ruefully, glancing over at the packed dance floor. "I'd feel an absolute idiot out there!"

"Give it a try, Yale. Please?"

"Where did you learn to pout so endearingly?" he inquired wryly.

"I'm not pouting, I'm being persuasive!" Dara snapped, slightly miffed at the comment.

"I beg your pardon," he said quickly, laughter in the hazel eyes. "I didn't mean to imply you were one of those annoying females who gets her way by threatening to sulk."

"Yes, you did, but I'm going to ignore it. I'm too anxious to get you out onto the dance floor."

"Why?" Yale tossed her an unexpectedly stark look which vanished almost immediately.

"Because I like to dance, of course. Why do you think I brought you here?" Dara smiled dazzlingly.

"You wanted to make me feel uncomfortable? Out of my element?" he guessed coolly.

"No!" But there was a trace of guilt behind the word, and Dara was afraid she might not have hidden it with complete success. She did want to jar him a little, watch him react to a situation where he could not hide behind his image. She felt an almost reckless urge to find out what lay behind that conservative, Southern-gentleman exterior.

"You're a little old to be playing games like this, aren't you?" Yale asked after a moment's thought.

"Games! I'm not playing games! You asked me to leave the party with you and then you asked me where I wanted to go dancing. I've been nothing but straightforward about the whole thing!"

He favored her with a narrow stare for a moment and then set down his beer abruptly. "All right. We'll dance."

"Now? But they've just changed to a slow number. I wanted—"

"You wanted to dance. I'm offering this one. Take it or leave it."

Dara got to her feet without further argument. "It really

is slipping, Yale. I feel in all fairness that I ought to warn you again," she whispered as he led her out onto the wooden floor and took her quite formally in his arms.

"My gentlemanly image?" he hazarded. "It's probably not surprising. You've been provoking me all evening. I wonder why. Did you think that getting my attention like this was the best way to go about getting my account?"

"Is it?" Dara leaned her head against his shoulder, forcing a closer intimacy than he had attempted.

"Beats me," Yale admitted, relaxing his grip and letting his body make contact with hers. "I guess we'll find out, won't we? What's wrong with my image, anyway?" He sounded interested.

"I don't know," Dara told him honestly, a slow smile quirking her mouth as she nestled her head against the expensive material of his jacket and closed her eyes. "Something about it isn't quite real."

"You don't believe I'm really an accountant?"

"Of course I believe you're an accountant! It's not that. . . ."

"Are you sleepy?" he asked suddenly, ignoring her comment.

Gray-green eyes flickered open and she met his slightly frowning look.

"A little. I've had a long day. Stockbrokers get up early, you know. I'm at the office by seven on weekday mornings. What's the matter? You don't like women falling asleep on your shoulder while you're dancing with them?"

"Not particularly."

"Then you should have danced a fast one with me. That would have perked me up considerably," Dara advised him.

"I'll remember that. In the meantime, try not to drift off completely, will you? I feel idiotic enough out here with all these fake cowboys. Carrying you off the floor isn't going to make me feel any more at home!"

"You sound annoyed," Dara told him, aware of the lean length of him as the dance grew a little more intimate. Strange how her soft curves seemed to fit the hardness of him. Was he responding to her? She couldn't be sure. There was an aloofness to Yale Ransom at the moment. As if he were deliberately trying to put some distance between them.

"Do I? Does that worry you?"

"Nope."

"Maybe it should," he suggested dryly.

"I'm not afraid of losing your account," Dara returned blithely.

"Edison, Stanford and Zane might not appreciate your losing it!"

"Am I in any danger of letting down the firm?" she taunted.

"You haven't got your hands on my money yet," he reminded her with a small smile.

"The evening's young," she teased.

"Perhaps, but you've already admitted you're in danger of falling asleep."

"So keep me awake. Tell me about yourself, Yale Ransom."

"Stop snuggling!" Yale muttered feelingly. "How old are you, anyway?"

"Too old to snuggle, I expect." Dara sighed. "I'm thirty. How old are you?"

"Thirty-seven," he answered shortly, as if his mind were on something else. "You're not married, are you? It would be just my luck to have an irate husband come barging in."

"Relax," she soothed. "I'm not married. Not anymore. Besides, I told you I'd take care of you in here, didn't I? Trust me."

"Not anymore," he repeated thoughtfully. "But you were once."

"Yes."

22

"What happened?"

"Do you really want to know?" she asked a little distantly.

"Yes," he said with sudden conviction. "I think I do."

"Six months into the marriage my husband realized he'd made a terrible mistake. Unfortunately for me, his ex-fiancée, who had broken off with him to marry another man, made the same discovery at about the same time." Dara shrugged philosophically. "It seemed my husband had been on the rebound when he set about sweeping me off my feet. When both he and his former lover realized they'd made a tragic error, there wasn't anything for them to do except apologize profusely to their respective spouses and ask for divorces."

There was a moment's silence above her head while Yale considered the brief story.

"You sound remarkably understanding," he finally said quietly.

"It all happened a long time ago," she said softly, opening her eyes to study the hard line of his jaw. "I don't think about it much anymore."

"But you haven't remarried, either."

"No. There are other things in life." She smiled. "What about you, Yale? Have you ever been married?"

"Yes."

She waited, and when no further information was forthcoming, Dara tried probing. "A long time ago?"

"Um-hmm."

"Before you became a Southern-gentleman accountant?"

"You are an inquisitive little thing, aren't you?" he charged with a stifled groan. His hold on her tightened, but Dara was inclined to think that it was more in irritation than anything else.

"I like to know my clients," she explained placidly, waiting with a hopeful expression for further details of his past.

"So you keep saying." Yale angled his head downward, the smoky light illuminating the honey-colored, neatly trimmed hair. "Are you sure you want to know so much about me?"

"Are you trying to warn me that I might not like what I discover?" She grinned.

"It's a possibility."

"Try me."

"It's tempting."

"I meant try telling me something about yourself!" Dara snapped tersely, mildly annoyed by his sexual interpretation of her words. Why did men always concentrate on the physical side of a budding relationship? Didn't they realize that there were more important matters between a man and a woman? Matters which should be dealt with before the physical side of things was explored?

"Oh."

She could almost feel him thinking it over and waited impatiently for his decision.

"Perhaps," Yale said slowly, "I ought to show you."

"Show me?" She tipped her head quizzically to one side as the dance drew to a close and they stopped moving.

"Mmm. How badly do you want to know me, Dara Bancroft?" he asked almost whimsically as he led her off the floor. His arm was wrapped rather casually around her waist, but Dara liked the feel of it.

"You make it all sound very mysterious," she countered impishly.

"It's not. It's just that no one's ever been so insistent about it. In fact," he told her with sudden decision, "I don't think anyone's ever even realized . . ."

"Realized what?" she pressed eagerly.

"Come on, my curious little tabby cat, and I'll show you." He grinned. The flashing gold tooth winked devilishly and Dara felt a small chill slip down her spine. What was she getting into by pushing Yale Ransom like this? One thing was certain. She couldn't stop now. She would spend the rest of her life wondering about him. She knew that much with crystal certainty.

It was unfortunate, though, she told herself wryly as he helped her back into her coat, that he thought of her as only a curious little tabby cat.

Without a word, Yale led her out of the glittering, rhinestone-cowboy nightclub.

2

᭙᭙᭙᭙᭙᭙᭙᭙᭙᭙᭙

Are you crazy?" Dara laughed, half appalled as she realized their destination some fifteen minutes later. "That's a roadhouse! A truck stop! The *real* kind."

"Afraid?" Yale asked succinctly, glancing at the parking lot full of trucks, large and small, and cruising on past to a point almost two blocks farther along the street.

"Talk about feeling out of place!" Dara exclaimed, ignoring his question. "What are you trying to prove?"

"I asked if you were afraid."

She thought about that a moment. "Well, no, not exactly. Not as long as you're with me, but . . ."

"I'll take that as a compliment." He grinned, parking the Alfa Romeo and climbing out.

"Why are we parking way down here? There was room in the lot." Dara watched, brow wrinkling in puzzled fashion as Yale slipped off his jacket and tossed it over the seat. His tie went next.

"Because I don't want to take a chance on coming

26

back and finding the car door accidentally kicked in," he explained as if she weren't very bright.

"Accidentally?" she murmured, climbing out of her side of the car and facing him across the roof. He was unbuttoning the top two buttons on his white shirt and rolling the sleeves.

"Accidents sometimes happen around places like this." Yale grinned.

She watched in growing fascination now as he removed his glasses and tucked them into a case in his shirt pocket. Then he raked a hand carelessly through his amber-shaded hair and the grin broadened. Gold gleamed in the moonlight.

"My God!" Dara breathed, her eyes full of laughter. "If I hadn't seen it with my own eyes I wouldn't have believed it!"

She turned as he walked around the hood of the car and came to stand beside her. Deliberately she ran an eye over him from head to foot.

"I can see that only one of us is going to feel out of place here," she finally groaned, shaking her head at the transformation. "You look like you just stepped off the rodeo circuit!"

"Don't worry about how you look," Yale told her consolingly. "I'll take care of you."

"You'd better! Remember that I didn't let anything terrible happen to you at *my* nightclub!" She slipped off her coat and left it behind.

"Trust me," he instructed, lacing her close to his side with a strangely possessive arm around her shoulders.

Dara shot him a quick glance from under her lashes at the familiarity of the grip but said nothing. In any event, her unspoken question was answered almost as soon as they stepped inside the loud, smoky tavern. Several male heads turned to run frankly sexual gazes over her rounded curves.

Dara felt like a prize palomino being led around an auction ring. This sort of inspection might be common in taverns and nightclubs the world over, but she was accustomed to it being performed in a more subtle manner. The crowd here was not subtle.

But the interested eyes always came to a halt when they took in the sight of the sinewy arm anchoring her to Yale's side. After one last, assessing glance at her companion most of the eyes turned back to other subjects, such as the beer on the table or the sultry female lead singer with the band. With a wry grimace, Dara admitted that the possessiveness in Yale's hold was purely for her own protection.

"I suppose there's a point to all this?" she forced herself to say flippantly as Yale found a table and settled her into a chair.

"My bringing you here? You asked for it. Remember that," he went on with a touch of grimness. "Whatever happens tonight, you asked for it!"

Some of her laughter fading, Dara stared at him. "Are you angry with me?"

He stared back for another moment. "I can't decide whether I am or not."

Dara bit her lip, suddenly contrite. Her gray-green eyes widened in genuine apology. "Yale, I'm sorry if I've made you show me something you didn't want to show me about yourself. I never meant—"

"Didn't you?" he asked cryptically, signalling the blond waitress for two beers. American beers, Dara realized vaguely. That was the only sort the bar featured.

"Well, I admit I was curious." She sighed ruefully. "But I still don't understand everything. What's the big mystery? That you're at home in places like this? What did you do for a living before you became an accountant?"

He leaned back in his chair and studied her anxious

expression. Dara would have given a great deal to know exactly what he was thinking.

"A lot of things," he finally said evenly, his eyes intent.

"You weren't raised on a charming, picture-book plantation with lots of history and money and the right Southern schools, were you?" Dara risked, her eyes smiling across the table at him. She willed him to respond, but he continued to watch her with that implacable gaze.

"Not quite," he said absently, fishing out cash for the impatient waitress. When she'd left with a fat tip, Yale finally seemed to come to a decision. "I was raised in the Blue Ridge Mountains. Know them?"

"North Carolina? Somewhere around Asheville?" At least he was talking, she thought hopefully.

He nodded.

"So?"

"So—" Yale drew a deep breath as if about to plunge into a cold pool—"I've spent a lot of time and effort leaving those damn mountains and all they stood for behind me. I've put a couple of thousand miles between me and them, as well as a college education and a better accent. I've changed almost everything I could change, and over the past several years I've built a very successful image. Then you come along and in the space of a couple of hours tear through all my fine plumage demanding to know the real me."

"I see," Dara whispered, guilt rising now that she began to realize exactly what she'd done. "But I don't understand why you bothered. You could have told me to mind my own business. You didn't have to ask me to leave the party with you. You didn't—"

"I don't know why I did it, myself," Yale said quietly. "Would you like to dance?"

"Yale, I think we ought to talk about this first," Dara began earnestly. "I mean, everyone knows that part of the country has a lot of poverty, but I don't see why you should be so determined to forget you came from there. Everyone also knows the mountain people have a lot of pride and courage and—"

"Are you going to dance with me or not?" he interrupted as if she hadn't spoken.

Dara sighed. He wasn't in the mood for a philosophical discussion of his origins. That much was obvious.

"Yes, I'd like to dance," she said softly, getting to her feet.

The band slipped into a twanging waltz, the singer crying out a song of unfaithful men who spent their nights in taverns like this one and left their women alone at home.

"I thought the mountain music was more of the bluegrass type," Dara couldn't resist saying as Yale took her into his arms.

"Sorry. This was as close as I could get. I'm sure the band knows a few bluegrass tunes," Yale told her shortly.

There was silence between them as they moved around the floor to the country waltz. Dara tried to think of something to say, anything to break the strange mood she had created. At least Yale was holding her closer now, she told herself with determined cheer. He might be a little angry at her, but he wasn't trying to keep her at a physical distance the way he had earlier. Nestling her head against his shoulder, she took advantage of that small concession.

But she couldn't keep silent long. The urge to know the full truth about her escort was overpowering.

"What *did* you do before you became an accountant?" she finally dared to ask softly, speaking into the fabric of his shirt. She felt his arms stiffen around her.

"You don't seem to know when you've pushed your luck far enough," Yale observed almost mildly above her head.

30

"I'm sorry," she murmured humbly. "I can't help it. I want to know."

"Are you this curious about all your potential clients?" he drawled. Some of the aristocratic Southern accent was fading to be replaced by a slightly different inflection. From the mountains? she wondered.

"No," Dara admitted honestly.

"I suggest you don't ask any more questions tonight, honey," Yale advised very gently. "You've gone far enough."

Dara raised her head and opened her eyes at the faint warning in his words. Yet another question hovered on her lips, and she was on the verge of asking it when a gleam of purely masculine impatience lit the hazel eyes gazing down into hers. Before she could get the words out of her mouth, Yale took action to silence her very effectively.

Bending his head, he took her lips with a slow, forceful possession that startled Dara into momentary blankness. For an instant she struggled instinctively, not so much against the kiss itself, but against having her next question cut off so completely.

He never missed a beat of the waltz as he tightened his arms, stilling her automatic protest. Then he placed the hand he was holding around his neck so that her arms were circling him in an intimate dancing posture. His fingers moved with deliberate exploration down her sides, into the curve of her waist, and came to a rest on the flare of her hips.

Telling herself that he was beginning to get out of line, Dara made a move to break off the kiss, but he diverted the effort by using his hands to press her close against the lower half of his body. His mouth moved tantalizingly on hers as he forced her into the hardness of his hips.

With growing shock, Dara finally realized she was being made love to in the middle of a dance floor. No one else seemed the least bit scandalized, she had to acknowledge. The other couples on the floor were equally involved with each other. But she wasn't used to this sort of public display, she told herself firmly, trying and failing once more to pull back.

Helplessly she found herself molded against Yale's lean length. She could sense the arousal growing in him, felt it in the deepening kiss which was threatening to swamp her senses. His tongue probed her bruised lips, seeking entrance to the warmth of her mouth.

Dara tried to remain firm in the face of the seductive invasion, telling herself this simply wasn't the place for that sort of thing, regardless of how inviting Yale made it seem. But his fingers began stroking the small of her back, finding the sensitive area at the base of her spine and massaging it sensuously.

"Oh, Yale," she groaned huskily against his mouth, and as she spoke the words he took advantage of the opportunity to force his way gently past her teeth.

The kiss exploded in heated sexual energy, destroying the last of her feeble defenses. Without another thought, Dara stopped trying to resist the impulse to simply let her full weight lean into the strength of him.

She felt her high, curving breasts crushed against the muscular chest, knew the power in Yale's thighs and felt his desire for her. It shocked her senses, sending answering thrills out to her fingertips, and she knew she was making small, helpless sounds deep in her throat.

When her arms tightened around his neck, Yale rasped her name into her mouth and she felt the tremor of barely hidden passion which went through him. He wanted her, she realized dazedly. He truly wanted her! All the hope and excitement which had blazed so unexpectedly into life earlier in the evening when she'd given him her hand in greeting was culminating in a sense of wonder. Who would have thought that she would have to wait until she was thirty to know this sensation . . . ?

Or that she would find it in the middle of a honky-tonk dance floor? the humorous side of her nature tossed in for good measure as Yale's hands slid down to follow the curve of her buttocks beneath the soft material of her dress. She shivered at the caress.

The twanging waltz came to a close and sensuously entwined dancers began making their way slowly off the floor as the strains of a toe-tapping railroad song took over.

Yale's arm guided her through the smoke-filled, dimly lit room, past a table of raucous truck drivers who watched in open male appreciation as she walked by them. Self-consciously, Dara kept her eyes on the far wall, grateful for Yale's possessive arm on her waist.

"I think we've got a visitor," Yale said calmly as they neared their table. The sound effects of a nearby electronic pinball game covered his next words, and Dara glanced up curiously. Then she saw the husky stranger sitting at their table.

The large man, balding on top and wearing a belt which had to be buckled below his stomach to accommodate his bulk, stood up at once as they approached.

"Sorry, folks." He grinned good-naturedly. "Tables are kind of scarce, and I was taking a chance this one might have been recently vacated." His bright blue eyes dropped interestedly to Dara's neckline with the appraising look she was coming to expect. "I'll be moving on," he added, picking up his bottle of beer. "Reckon there's always a spot at the bar. . . ."

"That's all right," Yale said easily, surprising Dara. "Why don't you join us for a while? We don't mind sharing, do we, Dara?"

Dara shook her head and smiled politely, thinking that Yale's accent seemed to be changing more and more quickly. He was beginning to sound a little like the truck driver who had just taken their table.

"I appreciate that, friend." Their new acquaintance

33

grinned, resuming his seat as Dara sat down. "I won't be staying long. Got a lot of miles ahead of me tonight."

"Where you headed?" Yale asked laconically, reaching for his beer.

"Sacramento."

"Home port?"

"You can say that again," the stranger breathed with an air of great expectation. "Got a wife and kid waitin' there. Name's Bonner, by the way. Hank Bonner."

Yale introduced himself and Dara, and when Hank's eyes strayed to her neckline, Dara felt obliged to try some sort of distraction.

"I, uh, expect your wife must miss you when you're gone on these long trips," she said gently. "I take it you drive a truck?"

"You take it right. And I surely hope to God she's been missing me!" Hank said in a heartfelt tone.

"How old is your child?" Dara persevered bravely, wishing he wouldn't look at her quite so interestedly.

"Two." Hank brightened suddenly. "Got a picture. Want to see it?"

"Oh, I'd love to." She smiled quickly.

She was aware of Yale's silent amusement as Hank Bonner began dragging photographs out of his wallet. He had several pictures, it seemed, of a smiling, dark-haired woman holding a young boy. He spread them out in front of Dara with obvious pleasure.

"Took this one out behind the house last month. That's the new camper I just bought, and this one's on the front lawn. Wife wanted that new patio furniture so bad I finally had to break down and get it for her," he said, shaking his head affectionately. "No peace at all until it arrived. Guess women are like that, huh, Ransom?" He grinned.

Yale's mouth lifted slightly at the corners. "I guess so. No peace at all until they get what they're after."

Dara ignored his sardonic glance, but she couldn't fully

34

ignore his next words. "The interesting part is watching them find out if they really wanted it after they've gotten it."

"I'd be willing to bet that women know their own minds better than men ever will!" she stated firmly, shooting Yale a severe glance.

"That's a fact!" Hank Bonner agreed, chuckling. "Probably ain't a man alive who really understands a woman's mind!"

"No great loss, I reckon, as long as he understands the rest of her," Yale said smoothly, sipping his beer and watching the color climb in Dara's cheeks.

"The man who doesn't make an effort to understand both is only going to get half the satisfaction out of a relationship!" she heard herself say crisply.

"But it's likely to be the half that counts," Yale retorted coolly while Hank roared with laughter. Dara glared at him.

"I like this little lady of yours, Ransom. Don't suppose you'd let me have a dance with her, would you?" Hank asked hopefully.

Dara winced. It was obvious her feelings didn't matter. As far as Hank was concerned, she was private property and he had to request permission from the owner, not the property!

Yale shrugged. "Ask her yourself. I guess she can do what she wants."

"I'll keep her safe and sound," Hank vowed, getting to his feet and clearly expecting Dara to do the same.

Thoroughly annoyed but not yet at the point where she was willing to cause a scene in such unfamiliar territory, Dara allowed herself to be led off by Hank Bonner.

"Where'd Ransom meet a little lady like you?" Hank asked glibly as he took her into his arms for another country waltz. "You come here often?"

"This is my first time here," Dara said politely. "As

35

you've probably already guessed," she added as Hank grinned broadly.

"No offense, ma'am, but you are a little different from the kind of woman I normally find here."

"Do I look so out of place?"

"Just different," he repeated soothingly. "So where did you meet Ransom if not here?"

"You mean he *does* look like he belongs here?" she asked immediately, curious once again. It would be helpful to have another opinion on the man, she thought.

Hank Bonner chuckled. "Sure. I'm just wonderin' where he had to go to find you, that's all."

"A party," Dara explained weakly.

"Must have been some party!"

Dara wisely let that one go and concentrated on following Hank's energetic waltzing. Eventually the dance came to an end and Dara turned with relief to head back to the table. Somehow, in spite of his less than gentlemanly behavior this evening, Yale represented safety in this strange place. She was turning that one over in her head when a very drunken cowboy loomed in her path.

"Is the lady beginnin' to circulate?" he drawled deliberately, dark eyes moving crudely over Dara. "It so happens I'm lookin' for a partner . . ." He stretched out a hand to snag her wrist and Dara instinctively withdrew, bumping against Hank's protruding stomach. His arm came around her protectively.

"Sorry, the lady's only on temporary loan to me. Got to return her to the rightful owner," Hank explained breezily. But Dara could feel the sudden tightening of his muscles.

Oh, Lord! she thought, horrified. She mustn't let this turn into a fight!

"Excuse me," she said very firmly. "I have to get back to my table."

"Come on, honey," the drunken cowboy said, his

words slurring as he tried once again for a grip on her wrist. "I dance a hell of a lot better than this turkey, and as long as your man's lettin' you entertain others . . ."

"Let go of me, you idiot!" Dara grated, pulling her hand free with a totally exasperated movement.

"You heard her," Hank growled, and now Dara knew beyond a shadow of a doubt that her dancing partner was preparing for battle.

Beginning to panic, she scanned the teeming crowd for Yale.

"Stop it, both of you," she tried in desperation. "I'm not going to dance with anyone . . . !"

"Except me," the cowboy muttered.

"Yale!" Instinctively, Dara put herself between the two men who seemed on the verge of a fist fight. "Yale! Where the . . . oh! There you are!"

She saw him as he suddenly appeared behind the cowboy and tore herself free of Hank's protection to hurl herself into Yale's arms.

"It's about time you showed up!" she hissed as he curved an arm around her waist and held her against his side.

"Didn't take you long to start causing trouble, did it?" he observed placidly, his eyes on the drunk. "A slight misunderstanding here?"

"Ah, he's just bombed out of his skull," Hank explained disparagingly, sauntering forward. "Thought Dara was spreading the favors around. I was about to set him straight, but now you're here I reckon that's your right."

"No one is going to set anyone straight!" Dara yelped angrily. "I'm not going to dance with anyone! Is that clear?"

"As crystal," Yale confirmed, grinning down at her. "Ready to sit down?"

"Yes!"

37

"Then, if you'll excuse us," Yale told the cowboy imperturbably, "we'll be on our way. Unless, of course," he added silkily, "you have some objection?"

Dara froze, realizing with appalled comprehension that Yale was as fully prepared to fight as Hank had been. What was the matter with these men? Was that the only solution they had to "misunderstandings" of this nature?

"Yale, please!" she whispered fiercely, tugging at his sleeve. He ignored her, his narrowed, waiting gaze on the cowboy.

"I thought she was being allowed off the leash," the drunken man muttered. "Not my fault . . ."

"As I said, a misunderstanding." Yale nodded pleasantly. But Dara could feel the tautness of his muscles and knew he was still coiled to strike. "I'm sure you can find another woman. This one's mine."

With a frustrated and angry glance at Dara, the man wheeled unsteadily and plunged off through the crowd.

"A sigh of relief?" Yale murmured, his fingers, which were resting just under her breast, correctly interpreting her long breath.

"You don't have to look so nervous, Dara," Hank told her soothingly. "Ransom ain't gonna let anything happen to you."

"I can't tell you how reassuring that is!" she snapped without thinking, her annoyance plain.

"Why are you so upset?" Hank demanded, genuinely puzzled. "You don't want to dance with that creep, and we're here to make sure you don't have to!"

"Just another example of not being able to understand a woman's mind, Hank," Yale quipped, pushing Dara gently back toward the table. "Do what you think she wants and help her out of a situation, and the first thing she does is lose her temper!"

"The temptation to knock both your heads together is rapidly becoming irresistible," Dara informed them grandly, taking her seat. "You might be able to defend me against drunken fools, but who's going to defend you against me?"

"She's got a point," Yale conceded, grinning at Hank.

"That she does," Hank agreed admiringly. "A good point like that deserves another beer. I'm buying!"

Dara reflected much later that they might all still have managed to get out of the tavern without a fight if the frustrated drunk hadn't decided to take out his anger on the pinball machine.

At least, she assumed that was what initiated the disaster. There was a loud, shattering sound from the direction of the game machines shortly after the arrival of the beers Hank had ordered.

"What in the world . . . !" Dara swung around to stare in the direction everyone else was staring, but it was impossible to see exactly what was happening. The group of men standing around the machines seemed to turn into a brawling riot before her very eyes.

"It would appear this enchanting evening is about to come to a close." Yale groaned, getting lithely to his feet as chaos erupted. The band played on, oblivious to the shouts and yells and bodies spilling onto the dance floor.

"Yale!" she squeaked, once more seeking the sanctuary of his smoothly muscled strength. "What's going on?"

"Guess," he invited succinctly, turning toward the door and shoving her unceremoniously in front of him. "'Bye, Hank. Nice meeting you. Have a good trip down to Sac. . . .'"

"Reckon I will at that," Hank agreed cheerfully, grabbing his jacket and loping after them as he tossed a vaguely regretful glance back over his shoulder at the rapidly expanding fight.

The sounds of breaking glass and male war calls were all around Dara as Yale hustled her through the mob. She gasped as the path which had appeared momentarily clear toward the door was suddenly littered with brawling men.

"This way," Yale ordered, pulling her off course in an attempt to circle the melee.

"What the hell you think you're doin', pal?" Hank's voice demanded behind them.

Dara felt Yale hesitate and then turn to see what had happened to Hank. She swiveled with him, and both were in time to watch their table partner deflect a swinging beer bottle with his jacket-wrapped arm. An instant later he was planting a huge, square fist into the face of the man who had swung the bottle.

Before he could recover his balance, though, another man surged out of the mob, swinging a bottle. It was the drunken cowboy who had insisted on dancing with her, Dara realized dazedly.

She thought he was going to bring the bottle down on Hank's balding head, but before that could happen, Yale had left her side to intercept.

Hands across her mouth in the traditional pose of feminine shock, Dara gazed, stunned, as Yale stopped the drunk with an arcing fist. The drunken cowboy sank to the floor, blissfully unconscious.

"Hey, thanks, Ransom. That's one I owe ya." Hank beamed.

"Come on, both of you. Let's get out of here," Yale ordered, forcing his way once more toward the door.

From somewhere in the distance the wail of a police siren sounded.

"Some spoilsport must have called the cops," Hank muttered as the three of them made the door and staggered out into the parking lot. "Yup, here they come. Where you guys parked?"

"A couple of blocks away," Yale growled, grasping Dara's wrist and yanking her in the proper direction.

"You'll never make it, and they'll be lookin' for anyone

they can get their hands on. . . . Come on. My truck's out back!"

"Hank!" Dara exclaimed as she caught sight of a dark splotch on his hand. "What happened? You've been cut!"

"That bottle raked across my knuckles. Don't worry, I'll be all right."

"Driving's going to be tough," Yale gritted, pulling Dara along in his wake. "Want me to take over?"

"I'd appreciate it." Hank chuckled, nursing his injured hand. "That's my baby there." He pointed to a huge, gleaming tractor-trailer truck which stood like a monstrous prehistoric creature in the back parking lot.

"In you go, Dara," Yale said briskly, practically tossing her up into the cab and climbing in beside her on the driver's side. He started the engine as Hank bounced up into the seat beside Dara.

"Yale, do you think we should be doing this? I mean, you're not supposed to leave the scene of a crime, or something like that. We're witnesses . . ."

"Nobody but a fool would stick around a situation like that," Yale told her kindly, shifting the massive gears and setting the huge truck and trailer in motion. "Trust me, honey. I know what I'm doing. This is my element, not yours."

Ruefully acknowledging the truth of that, Dara subsided as the huge truck lumbered off into the night. Bemusedly she watched as the Interstate sign flashed past. Yale was taking them onto the freeway.

Belatedly she remembered Hank's hand.

"Have you got a first-aid kit? I should put something on that hand," she said, turning in concern.

"Somewhere around here . . ." he said, rustling about behind her in the sleeping compartment. "Say, you seem to know what you're doing there, Ransom. Still doing it for a living?"

"Not anymore," Yale replied, catching Dara's quick

41

glance out of the corner of his eye and grinning wickedly. "Kind of feels good to get my hands back on the wheel, though."

"Yeah, much as I complain about it, I'd miss it if I had to stop tomorrow," Hank said, dragging out a first-aid kit.

Dara opened it quickly, pulling out necessary supplies and going to work on the cut hand.

"I don't think it's too bad," she finally said, taping the wound carefully. "Be sure to change the dressing. I've tried to clean it up as best I can, but you should probably still have a doctor look at it."

"I'll be home tomorrow. My wife can check on it," Hank said unconcernedly. "Thanks for the patching job, though. Between the two of you, you've both been right useful tonight!"

"It's, uh, certainly been an adventure," Dara agreed carefully, slanting a greenish glance up at Yale's hard profile. He looked right at home. "How far are we going with Hank?" she asked softly.

"I don't know. Hadn't thought about it," Yale murmured. "Why don't you crawl in the back and catch some sleep? You were tired earlier this evening, so I expect you're exhausted by now."

"Yale," she whispered, "we can't just go off like this! What about your car? How will we get back to Eugene? Where are we headed, anyway?"

"Go to sleep, honey. I'll take care of everything," he instructed gently.

"Go on, Dara," Hank said soothingly. "Let your man have some fun. The sleeper's not as clean as it ought to be, but you'll be all right if you stay on top of the blankets."

"Fun?" Dara eyed her escort. "Are you enjoying this, Yale Ransom?" she asked accusingly.

"I don't know. Can't decide." He chuckled. "Stop looking at me like that and go to sleep. I'll wake you later."

Dara licked her lower lip in thoughtful contemplation. But she was outnumbered and she was exhausted. And she had brought the whole catastrophe down on her own head, she remembered in a surge of self-honesty. And it really had been rather exciting.

She smiled slowly to herself and climbed obediently into the sleeping compartment. Yale could handle everything.

3

Where are we?"

Dara's voice was a sleepy mumble as she stirred awake some time later. It was the lack of the muted roar of the heavy diesel engine which had roused her, and she realized the big rig had been stopped.

"A couple of hours south of Eugene." Yale's voice came calmly from the front seat. "Come on, honey, this is where we get off."

"A couple of hours south! Good grief! How are we going to get back tonight?" she demanded, scrambling out of the sleeper compartment. She was aware that the burnt russet of her hair was tousled and the emerald dress was badly wrinkled. The sleeping compartment had been strangely confining and she was glad to escape, even if she was still very sleepy.

"We'll worry about that in the morning," Yale told her, reaching out to help her back into the front seat. His mouth quirked in amusement as she blinked up at him sleepily. "You look like a tabby cat someone's just rudely awakened."

"Thanks," she muttered, knowing tabby cats tended to be plump and comfortable-looking, not sleek and racy. "How's the wound, Hank?" she added, eyes narrowing as she turned to peer at the other man's hand.

He held it up and grinned cheerfully. "Fine. The bleeding's stopped and I can manage things now."

"Oh. Well, I hope you have a good, safe trip on down to Sacramento," she said, returning his smile. "And . . . and I think you ought to consider finding another sort of job, Hank," she went on in an urgent rush. "This isn't a good life for a family man! Your wife shouldn't have to be raising that boy alone and—"

"Come on, Dara!" Yale's crisp drawl cut across the flow of words as he opened the door and grabbed her wrist. She was practically pulled down out of the cab and he had to steady her as she landed off balance beside him.

Hank's face appeared in the window above them as he slid behind the wheel. He was grinning.

"You take care of that little lady, now, Ransom. She looks to me like she's got about everything a man could want on a cold night! See ya!"

Yale wrapped an arm around Dara's waist and pulled her back out of the way as Hank brought the monster truck to life once more.

"Thanks, Hank," Yale called, lifting a hand in farewell.

"Anytime, pal, anytime!"

Diesel fumes filled the air as the truck and trailer growled past on its way back to the only element in which it was truly comfortable, an Interstate highway.

"It's cold out here!" Dara noted, wishing she hadn't left her coat in the Alfa Romeo. She glanced around at the scattered buildings.

"There's a motel over to the right," Yale said conversationally, holding her close to his side and starting off in the direction of the flashing sign advertising rooms.

"A motel!" Dara frowned. "Aren't we going to head back to Eugene?"

"Not tonight. We'll find a way back home in the morning. It's too late tonight to scare up a ride and we're both tired."

"What time is it?"

"Almost two o'clock. Did you get any sleep?"

"Between Hank fiddling with the CB and you switching from one country station to another on the radio, no!" Dara lied feelingly. "And what's the idea of telling half the northbound traffic on the Interstate that you were traveling with your own personal stockbroker?"

"I didn't tell anyone that. That was Hank on his CB," Yale defended with a grin that exposed the gold.

"He got it from you!"

"Well, he wanted to know your status in my life so he could share the gossip with his road buddies. I had to think of something."

Dara was about to berate him further, but the truth was she had fallen asleep shortly after hearing Hank's cheerful announcement and she wasn't at all sure what had been said next.

"Do you think this place is clean?" she demanded skeptically, surveying the old motel with a critical eye.

"Hank assures me it's fine. Not elegant, but decent."

"We're going to look a little strange to the desk clerk." Dara sighed, lifting a hand to graciously cover a yawn. Even the chilly night air wasn't going to keep her awake much longer. "I mean, what with no luggage and no car . . ."

"I'll handle it."

"Uh-huh."

"Have some faith in your man, woman!" Yale gibed cheerfully as he opened the front door of the office.

"I'm your stockbroker, not your woman, remember?" she retorted sweetly.

"Actually, we haven't even agreed on that status yet, have we?" he noted. The door swung shut behind them, cutting off her next words.

A thin, elderly desk clerk detached himself from a small television set and came forward reluctantly.

"Can I help you?" he asked, not looking particularly anxious to do so.

"Two rooms, Yale," Dara remembered to hiss belatedly in his ear as he loosened his arm and started toward the desk. He ignored her, but the desk clerk didn't.

"Only got one. A double. Take it or leave it, and you pay in advance," the thin man growled with an owlish glance at Dara.

"We'll take it," Yale said quickly, fishing his wallet out of his pocket. Swiftly he counted out the money and collected the key. He had signed the register and hustled Dara out the door before she fully realized what had happened.

"I told you to get two rooms!" she gritted as the office door slammed shut behind them.

"You heard the man. He only had one!"

"Hah!"

"Don't take that tone with me," Yale instructed, sounding aggrieved. "Our being in this situation is all your fault!"

"My fault! Of all the nerve! It wasn't me who got involved in a fight in a sleazy bar, and it wasn't my idea to hitch a ride with a long-distance trucker and not get out of the truck for two solid hours! If we'd stayed at that nice country-western place I took you to earlier this evening, none of this would have happened!"

"Don't act the innocent victim," Yale muttered, sliding the motel key into the lock of number 53. "You had to keep pushing at me, trying to find out what was under my

47

nice accountant image. You have only yourself to blame!"

"Oh, my God!" Dara breathed in grim resignation as the door swung open to reveal a stark but clean room. "There's only one bed. Where are you going to sleep?"

"On my side, naturally," Yale growled, closing the door behind them and switching on the light.

Since she had guessed the answer to the question before she'd even asked it, Dara squelched a retort. There wasn't much else she could do under the circumstances, and in spite of his almost blatant lovemaking on the dance floor earlier in the evening, Yale didn't look particularly amorous at the moment. And there was absolutely nothing romantic about the cheap, poorly furnished motel room.

"I'll use the bathroom first." She sighed gloomily.

Inside the spartan bath, Dara studied herself wryly in the mirror. She looked a little the worse for wear, she was forced to conclude, raking her fingers through her hair. Sleepy gray-green eyes gleamed back at her and she frowned as she realized there was a tiny hint of excitement in her own reflection.

Things hadn't developed quite the way she had imagined, but there was no denying she had found herself in an interesting situation. She grabbed a washcloth and began scrubbing her face while she considered that. Yale Ransom was turning out to have several fascinating layers. Surely after their shared experiences this evening he would feel a degree of friendship for her.

Perhaps enough friendship to give her his securities account. That would provide the excuse she needed to cement the relationship along business lines, and from there . . .

Dara broke off her hopeful thoughts and told herself not to get carried away. There was still a lot she didn't know about Yale. She wasn't even sure how he felt about her at the moment, although, judging from his reaction on the dance floor, she didn't leave him cold. Well, that was something, at least.

Hanging the threadbare white towel back on the rack, Dara unzipped the emerald-green dress and removed her lacy bra. Rolling the undergarment into a little bundle, she stuffed it into her purse and then rezipped the dress. It would be more comfortable trying to sleep without the bra, she told herself, wishing she could take off the dress, too. But that, of course, was impossible.

Yale was sitting on the side of the bed, his weight putting an alarming sag in the old mattress as he leaned over to untie his shoes. He had removed the white shirt and was wearing only his slacks.

"Your turn," Dara said cheerfully, determined to act with the casual comradeship the situation demanded. Damned if she would let him see her act like a nervous female! Not at her age!

He straightened, kicking off the dark leather shoes. The case containing the horn-rimmed glasses rested on the nightstand. His hazel eyes swept over her as she industriously began turning down her side of the bed.

"Thanks," he murmured, getting to his feet.

In spite of herself, Dara's gaze followed him as he disappeared into the bathroom. The broad shoulders and smoothly muscled back tapering into a narrow waist pulled at her awareness. She remembered how it had felt dancing with him earlier this evening and wondered at her own reaction. Never had she been so immediately attracted to a man.

Shaking her head, Dara slipped off her high-heeled shoes and panty hose and slid beneath the covers. Very carefully she arranged herself on the far side of the bed and lay on her back, gazing at the ceiling. Was there such a thing as love at first sight? she wondered. Probably not. But until tonight she wouldn't have expected to encounter attraction at first sight, either.

And attraction was a good place to start, she assured herself with a small smile, provided it was mutual.

"Don't tell me you're going to sleep in that dress!" Yale exclaimed, emerging from the bathroom and flicking off the overhead light as he walked toward the bed.

"As I didn't think to bring a nightgown, that's exactly what I'm going to do," Dara told him acidly and then winced as she heard the sound of a buckle and zipper being undone.

"Suit yourself," he remarked carelessly. She listened anxiously as he slung the dark slacks over a chair. A moment later the bed sagged once again and the large male body moving in beside her raised the temperature under the cold covers by several degrees.

"The least you could do is wear your slacks," she said in brisk annoyance, lying rigidly on her side of the bed as he shifted and stretched beside her.

"In order to keep warm, you mean?" Yale asked politely and reached for her with shocking swiftness. "That's what my own personal stockbroker is for," he informed her, dragging her into the curve of his body.

"Yale! Stop that! What in the world do you think you're doing?"

Dara flung out a hand in protest and encountered the pelt of curling hair on his chest. She pulled her fingers away as if they'd been burned. "Stop teasing me like this!"

"Teasing!" he growled, his arm moving around her waist to anchor her against him. "You're the tease in this little party. You've been badgering me all evening, and I've finally decided to give you what you want."

"I'm not in the mood for any more of your truck-stop manners!" she snapped haughtily. "You've had your fun tonight. Behave yourself!"

The hand on her waist slid around to her stomach and moved upward to settle just under the full curve of her breast.

"So you don't like my truck-stop manners? That's unfortunate, isn't it? You didn't seem to like my more gentlemanly behavior, either. You're a hard woman to please, Dara Bancroft. But I'll try. . . ."

Dara opened her lips to annihilate him verbally, but his mouth came down on hers before she could get the words out.

"Yale!" she managed in a muffled voice, and then the heated mastery of his kiss overwhelmed her senses. His mouth was like a narcotic, she realized dimly. A drugging, overridingly powerful thing that roused her emotions as nothing else had ever done. If she didn't stop him soon, she wouldn't be able to do so.

His fingers followed the under curve of her breast, seeking the nipple and finding it easily. She should have left on her bra, Dara thought wretchedly. Now his hand was shaping the softness of her as if the dress she wore were only a nightgown. The sensations he was causing began undermining her will power, urging compliance.

"Hank was right," Yale said huskily against her throat as he dragged his mouth away from hers. "You have got what a man needs in bed."

"Don't talk to me like that, Yale. We both know you've come a long way from the kind of world where men treat women like this!"

"I've got news for you, honey," he murmured, letting the tip of his tongue touch the rapidly beating pulse at the base of her throat. "Some things a man doesn't leave behind."

"No!" she gasped as he pulled her against his naked chest and reached for the zipper at her nape. "You're a gentleman, damn it! I'm holding you to that!"

His fingers hesitated, the zipper halfway open. "What makes you think I would have behaved any differently if I'd gotten you into bed tonight while I was still in my gentlemanly role?" His lips burned on her earlobe now, and she wedged her hands against the strong chest.

"We would never have wound up in bed like this if you hadn't taken over the evening!" Dara wailed.

"I really don't feel like arguing over whose fault this is," he soothed, lowering the zipper sensuously down to the base of her spine. "And don't try telling me you don't want me. I know what you were doing to me on that dance floor back at the bar and I know how you were responding."

"You don't understand!"

That brought a deep laugh from the back of his throat. "I understand, honey. Don't worry about that!" His fingers danced wickedly up her spine as she struggled futilely to lever herself away from his chest. When they reached her naked shoulder, the bold fingertips slid under the fabric of the dress bodice and pushed it forward, exposing the rounded femininity beneath.

Dara gasped, knowing that by now both his eyes and her own were adjusted to the darkness. He could see what his hands had revealed.

"Yale! Stop it! Please!" The cry was torn hoarsely from her throat as he lowered his dark amber head to taste the sweetness of her breasts. Her fingers curled unconsciously into the muscles of his shoulders and she heard him groan.

"You don't mean that," he rasped, his tongue circling a nipple, urging a physical response.

"Yes! Yes, I do, damn you! Please, Yale. This isn't the way I wanted things to be between us. It's too soon. We have to get to know each other. I want you to . . ." Her words trailed off. How could she tell him she wanted his love, not merely his desire? He would never understand how she could have fallen so completely for him in such a short period of time.

"You want me to what, sweetheart?" he whispered deeply, his teeth closing gently around the nipple his tongue had drawn forth. "Tell me. I'm willing to please. . . ."

"I want you to stop making love to me!" She was lying through her teeth but she spoke the words with considerable forcefulness.

He stilled for an instant and Dara, too, froze, waiting for his reaction. When his head eventually lifted and his eyes met hers with a directness that sent a shiver through her limbs, Dara almost called back her own words. Almost but not quite. The future was what mattered between them. To preserve that she had to protect the present.

"Are you sure that's what you want, honey?" he murmured coaxingly, his hand softly cupping one breast.

"I'm . . . I'm sure," she vowed, unable to look away from the seductive expression in the hazel gaze. "Please, Yale."

"I'll bet you sell a lot of stock with that earnest little look, don't you?"

"Yale!"

He sighed. "You're old enough to know better than to play with fire, Dara."

"I never meant things to get so out of hand," she said contritely. "I only wanted to know more about you and somehow . . ."

"Couldn't resist opening Pandora's box, could you?" He grinned, leaning back against the pillows. She felt the sexual tension seep out of him and drew a deep breath of relief—relief tinged with regret, she was forced to admit privately.

"Was all this in the nature of teaching me a lesson?" she complained ruefully.

"No," Yale growled, rubbing the bridge of his nose with his thumb and forefinger. "I suppose I'd forgotten a few of the things that were still in the box, myself." His eyes closed and suddenly he looked tired.

"How long did you drive a truck, Yale?" Dara asked, knowing quite suddenly that she was safe.

The amber lashes flicked open immediately and hazel

53

eyes gleamed in warning. "You really don't know when to stop, do you? Your curiosity must have gotten you into a lot of trouble over the years!"

"Not really. I've never been quite this curious about another person before!" she confessed.

He stared at her for a moment and then growled a soft command. "Go to sleep, Dara."

A little belatedly, perhaps, Dara acknowledged that it *was* time to stop. Without another word, she pulled away from the inviting proximity of his body, her hand brushing awkwardly against the material of his jockey shorts. Curling on her side with her back to him, Dara forced herself to stare at the wall until her eyes finally closed in sleep.

But her dreams were filled with fleeting promises of a happiness she craved, a happiness connected with a hazel-eyed man with honey-amber hair. In sleep her body remembered the feel of his hands, the strength of his chest and thighs and the laughter which sparked to life occasionally in the hazel gaze. There had never been a man like this one in her life, and he had even managed to invade her dreams.

It wasn't the morning sun which called Dara out of a warm sleep some time later. The shabby little motel room was still quite dark. It was a dream which was moving her into a drowsy, languid state of awareness. A dream which had followed her back into real life.

Half asleep, Dara's body reacted luxuriously to the warmth of a hand on her thigh. She knew that hand. She would know its touch anywhere, and her body accepted it instinctively.

Blissfully she turned toward the source of the gentle, insistent demand, her legs parting of their own volition. The half-conscious feminine invitation was accepted immediately. The hand on her leg began lazy designs which led to the soft inside of her thigh and simultaneously her mouth was warmly, tenderly invaded.

It was like drinking hot spiced wine, she thought dazedly, her arms moving to pull closer the source of this smooth, heated seduction. Her fingers closed first on the hard thrust of a shoulder and then they twined themselves into short, thick hair. Hair that she knew intuitively was the color of dark honey. The perfect shade.

"Oh . . ." The moan was from her own throat, thick with a growing urgency. It was as if her dream was merging with reality.

The masculine groan which echoed her soft cry was low and hoarse with undisguised male need. She responded to it, offering herself in an age-old desire to please.

There were no words. Somehow, far back in her foggy mind, Dara knew words would have destroyed the dreamlike quality of the moment, and nothing on earth must be allowed to do that.

There was a curious floating sensation as the material which seemed to interfere with the searching movements of the demanding hands was slipped away. When it was gone, Dara felt the glowing sensation increase a hundredfold. This was what she wanted; this was where she wished to be tonight and every night.

Eyes closed, she let the accumulating impressions pile up on her senses. Gently rough fingertips glided along the inside of her thigh until they closed on the heart of her throbbing desire. The electricity coursed through her veins, causing her nails to bite deeply into a taut male shoulder and score their way down to a lean waist.

Silently she called his name over and over, and then the word was a low, audible moan on her lips. It was the only word allowed in that moment out of time.

"Yale, oh, my darling, Yale!"

"Dara, sweet, womanly Dara. I knew you were dangerous the instant I met you! And now it's too late. Much too late. . . ."

The husky confession pleased her enormously and

Dara curled closer, her hips arching into the touch of his possessive hand, trading her feminine secrets for the satisfaction Yale could provide.

"Yes, sweetheart," he growled, his lips moving down her throat, pausing to caress her breasts and then trailing down even farther to bury themselves in her curving midsection. "Give yourself to me tonight. I want all of you. All you have to give. . . ."

She gasped as he dipped a wet kiss into her navel and then moved on, stringing kisses along the flare of a hip. His hand slipped down to grasp an ankle, tenderly forcing her legs even farther apart, and then she felt his teeth first feather and then nip the vulnerable inner length of her thigh.

Convulsively, her fingers locked in the dark honey of his hair and her body lifted into his urgent, demanding lips and hands.

"Oh, Yale. Please, please . . ."

"Tell me what you want," he rasped thickly, sliding his hands under her buttocks and holding her body still while he rose to settle himself between her legs. "Tell me, Dara!"

The command was punctuated by tiny, velvet kisses along her stomach.

"Love me, Yale!" The cry was a feminine order of the first magnitude. "Please, please make love to me!"

He inched slowly upward, his hands sliding along her waist to palm her breasts as his mouth explored her silky skin in their wake. She was vividly aware of the heavy maleness of him, knew it would soon pour over her in a wave.

Hungrily she wrapped her arms around him, drawing him down into her waiting body. Her lips buried themselves in his throat as he loomed over her and she clutched at the tensely muscled back.

"I knew it had to end like this between us tonight,"

Yale gasped, shuddering as her hands clung to him, dragging him under into the rippling tide of her. "Sooner or later it had to end like this. . . ."

"Yes, oh, yes," she panted, her breath coming in short, excited gasps that lifted her full breasts and crushed them softly against his chest.

Somehow it wasn't until she actually felt his unmistakable hardness against her that the last of the dream finally faded. Perhaps it was the stunning sensation of imminent masculine possession, or perhaps it was because she finally opened her eyes and took in the full significance of the cheap motel room. Whatever the cause, Dara was finally, fully aroused from her dreamlike state.

What was she doing? This wasn't the way she had meant to conclude the evening! It was too soon, much too soon! They needed time. . . .

"Yale, no! Wait, please, wait! I didn't want this to happen . . . !"

"It's too late now," he gritted against her mouth. "I'm going to make you mine. There's nothing in this universe that could stop me!"

He fastened his lips over hers, silencing her protest, and then everything seemed to explode around and in her at once. He held her with fierce urgency, forcing his tongue into her mouth even as his hardness took her completely.

Dara would have cried out with the ecstasy of it, but there was no chance. He dominated her awareness on every level, pulling her into the rhythmic surge of his body as if he would meld every inch of her with him.

Dara's fleeting moment of sanity vanished once more under the passionate onslaught. She couldn't think of the future when he held her like this, touched her like this, mastered her body with his own.

Deliriously she gave herself up to the thrilling wonder of the man to whom she had wanted to belong from the instant her eyes had met his. This was what she had been searching for all her life. This was the joy and exquisite excitement that had been missing from her short, ill-fated marriage.

Almost incredulously she felt her body responding in a way it had never responded before. Something tight and coiling was fighting to free itself deep in her loins.

Her hands slid down the violently arching male back, digging into the muscular flesh of Yale's buttocks and thighs.

"My God, woman! What are you doing to me!"

She reveled in the evidence of his unleashed need and sensuality, delighted in the now ungoverned response of his body to hers. His strength and power seemed to master her softness at the same time that they surrendered to it.

"I never knew . . ." she tried to say, "I never realized . . ." The words wouldn't come. How could she try to describe the indescribable?

Her teeth sank into his shoulder and her legs tightened violently around his rough thighs as the coiling passion in her lower body threatened to burst forth.

"Yale? Yale!" It was a plea. For what, she didn't know.

"Let yourself go, my darling," he whispered urgently. "I'll take care of you. Just let go. . . ."

Unable and unwilling to resist the demand in him, Dara gasped, reacting unbelievably to an unexpectedly swift and erotic movement of his lean frame. It seemed to send her over the brink of a heretofore unseen cliff and she plunged into the chasm below, free-falling toward a velvet green earth, Yale's name on her lips.

As if he had only been waiting for the turbulent shudder which suddenly racked Dara as she lay beneath him, Yale cried out harshly. She felt the primitive convulsion take him completely in its power, giving him to her in an astonishing and fundamental way.

Willingly, joyously, Dara accepted the gift, clinging and clinging as together they plunged into the soft valley below. He was with her in that moment, sharing the ultimate sensation which can be created between a man and a woman, and for Dara, that was all that counted. The future must be dealt with later.

4

~~~~~~~~~~~~~~~~

Languidly Dara attempted to move her foot, found it trapped beneath a heavy male leg and finally emerged completely from the sensual lethargy in which she had been drifting.

Her fingertips brushed a masculine chest and her soft gray-green eyes fluttered open to find a lazy pair of hazel ones watching her.

For an instant of silent communication, neither said anything, the recent memories mirrored in their eyes.

"I thought you were never going to wake up, sleepy-head," Yale finally murmured, his voice a deep dragon's purr in his chest. "It's been daylight for nearly an hour."

"You're in a hurry to go someplace?" Dara drawled, her mouth curving lovingly.

"Well, it did occur to me that there might be more interesting places to spend the weekend than this truck-stop motel!"

With a sexy, inviting grin, Yale rolled onto his back and reached out to haul her across his chest. It was as she came free of the sheet that Dara realized the green dress was no longer around.

The color rose in her cheeks as her breasts were crushed softly against him. She saw his eyes follow the outline of her, a look of satiated pleasure in the hazel depths.

"You drove me wild last night," he rumbled, raking his fingers through the tangled wings of her deep russet hair. "You're a dangerous lady, Dara Bancroft. Very dangerous."

She smiled delightedly, toying with the curling hair beneath her hand as she met his gaze. She was in love! She could hardly believe it. How could it have happened like this after all these years?

"I plead innocent," she whispered laughingly. "You're the one who carried me off into the night. If we'd done things my way we would have danced a few dances at that nice nightclub I took you to and then gone home very properly to our own beds!"

"Never!" he vowed fervently. "I wanted you from the moment I met you. Whatever happened last night, we would never have awakened alone."

"Hah! I don't think you wanted me all that badly at first. As I recall, you were rather annoyed with me at times!" Deliberately she made a joke of it, wishing he could have used the word she wanted to use. He must feel something more than desire for her after what they had shared. How could a man make love like that and not be at least a little *in* love?

"Being annoyed with you didn't change my desire to take you to bed." He chuckled, framing her face with his hands. Dara felt the strength in the gentle grip and shivered with pleasure. "I don't think anything could change that!"

"No?" she dared lightly, eyes warm with her love and laughter and the freshness of what she had discovered.

"No," he agreed solemnly. "Rest assured, my sweet. The account is yours."

Dara blinked, certain she had heard wrong.

"What?" Firmly she kept her smile in place. He was making a joke.

"My stock account," Yale explained easily, laughing at her incomprehension. "It's yours. I'm entirely satisfied with the transaction. At the moment, in fact, I wouldn't care if you lost all my money in the commodities market! As long as you're willing to stand as collateral, naturally."

"Stop teasing me like that, Yale," she ordered carefully, some of the laughter fading from her eyes. "I'm not in the mood for that sort of joke. Not right now."

"What joke?" he demanded, shaking his head ruefully. "It's yours, honey, me and the account. I'm content with the deal and as far as I'm concerned it's all signed, sealed and delivered. I'll let you have the details you'll need to transfer it from my broker in L.A. on Monday. But right now we've got today and Sunday ahead of us to, uh, finalize the terms of our working relationship. What do you say we—"

"You're not joking, are you?" Dara pushed herself a few inches away from his chest, gray-green eyes widening as she stared down into his fiercely etched face as if she hadn't fully seen it until that moment.

"I never joke about money. Accountants rarely do!" he informed her loftily, eyes narrowing a fraction as he studied her tautening expression.

"Oh, my God!" she breathed as the full horror of the situation washed over her. He wasn't teasing her! He really believed she had slept with him in order to convince him to give her his account!

"What's the matter with you, little tabby cat?" he rasped soothingly, stroking a rough fingertip down her cheek and into the curve of her shoulder. "I had the impression you were quite satisfied with last night's deal, too! In fact, I'd be willing to bet from the startled look on your face at one point that you hadn't known just how much pleasure you could find in your own body!"

"How dare you look so smug and self-satisfied! Who the hell do you think you are?" The words were tight, tense, barely audible.

Slowly at first the anger kindled. Fed by her own humiliation, it leaped to life, shattering Dara's conception of herself as a mild, easygoing person with an even temper. After thirty years, she was finally discovering the full significance of the red in her hair.

"Dara!" The command was given as if she were a fractious child. "Calm down . . . !"

"Calm down!" she blazed, pulling free of his hand and fumbling her way off the bed to stand beside it, glowering down at the man she had fallen in love with during the course of one wild night.

"Calm down! Don't you dare tell me to calm down!"

Yanking a sheet off the bed and leaving Yale's sprawling form nude in the morning light, she wrapped herself in some semblance of dignity. The gray-green eyes were almost completely emerald now and the sun seeping in through the crack in the curtains danced in the half-hidden fire of her hair.

"You are a bastard, Yale Ransom!" she proclaimed as if pronouncing a curse. "And I am a fool! I freely admit that! God only knows where I got the idea we could . . . could mean something important to each other. Believe it or not, I'm usually a better judge of men than this! I haven't made a mistake of this magnitude since I thought the man I was marrying was in love with me!"

"Dara, stop it! You're behaving like a shrew. It doesn't suit you, little tabby cat. Come back to bed and let me show you. . . ." Yale stretched out a hand, groping for her wrist.

"Don't you dare touch me, you arrogant, lying, *impostor!*" She moved back out of reach.

"Impostor!" For some reason he seized on that, mouth hardening ominously as he slowly sat up.

"Yes! Impostor! Cheat! Opportunist! The language isn't rich enough to supply all the words I need to describe you!" she gritted furiously. "Oh, I knew you were something other than what you were pretending to be last night. I knew you'd been a lot of other things besides an accountant, but I never guessed you were the kind of man who would use a woman and then pay her off by handing over money or . . . or your stock-market account!"

"Shut up and listen to me, you little wildcat," he grated, getting slowly to his feet. The hazel gaze flickered as she automatically backed out of reach.

"Don't get the idea I'm a bigger fool than I've already shown myself to be!" Dara cried, her chin lifting defiantly. "Listening to you was what got me into this mess! I don't intend to listen to you again! Ever! I try to learn from my mistakes, Yale Ransom. And you can rest assured you've just taught me one hell of a lesson! Even I can't quite believe how I could have made such an idiot of myself!"

"Good God! You're really intent on playing the woman scorned this morning, aren't you? But I haven't scorned you, honey. Just the opposite!"

"You've treated me like a . . . a commodity you could buy or sell," Dara hissed. "Last night you felt like buying it. Who knows? Tomorrow you might feel like selling it! What will you do then? Try to find another female broker who seems willing to pay the price? Let me give you a word of advice. Find someplace besides a dingy truck-stop motel to 'finalize' the deal. And the next morning, refrain from talking about the bargain itself until after breakfast. Much more civilized!"

"The choice of surroundings was yours!" Yale suddenly snapped, his fists planted on his hips. He stood in front of her, uncompromisingly naked and intimidatingly male.

The deep amber hair was ruffled into a rakish, dangerous-looking style and the hazel eyes gleamed with determination. The Southern accent had lost most of its polish.

"There certainly isn't much to your gentlemanly veneer now, is there?" Dara taunted, her rage threatening to overwhelm her. "I even get the blame for choosing a cheap, one-night-stand sort of motel! Well, I suppose that's the proper setting, after all. A one-night stand is certainly all this affair is ever going to amount to!"

"The hell it is! I've got news for you, Dara Bancroft! You handed yourself over to me, lock, stock and barrel, last night. It's too late now to back out!"

"Don't be so anxious to conclude the bargain," she warned scathingly. "If I ever got my hands on your account I'd pump every last dime into surefire losers! I'd take great pleasure in ruining you! You're damned right I'm feeling like a woman scorned, and just remember hell hath no fury like one! Give me a chance and I'll pay you back a hundredfold for what you did to me last night!"

"Your warning is duly noted," he drawled, stalking forward with slow, deliberate strides.

"Don't come any closer!" she ordered seethingly, holding the sheet in place as she backed away. "I mean it, Yale! I don't want you touching me. Not ever!"

"But I'm going to touch you," he promised with silky menace. "Often and in the most delightful places. You belong to me now, temper and all. Like I said, I'm satisfied with the transaction, and I'll make sure you are, too. . . ."

Dara came up against the wall, her eyes blazing as she realized she was trapped. "You really can't get it through that thick head of yours that I didn't go to bed with you in order to get your account, can you? Well, try writing it on the blackboard a few hundred times. Because I didn't! I don't want your account! I never cared one way or the other about it!"

"Too bad, because you're stuck with it," he gritted, his fingers curling over her bare shoulders. He pulled her away from the wall, close to his naked strength. "And believe me, I'll take every dollar you lose out of your soft hide." His mouth curled devilishly. "But I will also be very generous with my thanks for every dollar you make, too!"

"Take your hands off me!"

"I can't," he confessed almost ruefully. "I only have to look at you and I want to touch you. Stop fighting me, honey. You know as well as I do that what we found together last night was very, very good. I'll admit we rushed into things, but—"

"*We* rushed into things!" she yelped, incensed at the blithe accusation. "*I* had nothing to do with it! You're the one who hitched a ride for us to the middle of nowhere! You're the one who got us one room in a sleazy motel when I told you to get two! You're the one who assumed that just because we were forced to share a bed, I would let you make love to me! You're the one who seduced me while I was asleep, long after I'd made it clear I had no intention of going that far! You took advantage of me! And you ignored me at the last moment when I finally realized what was happening and told you to stop!"

"Of course I ignored you," he murmured, bending his head to brush his mouth affectionately across her forehead and then the tip of her nose. "You'd really have been angry at me this morning if I hadn't!"

"You're despicable!" She brought up a hand, wedging it against his chest and trying to shove him away. It was like pushing the Rock of Gibraltar.

"What if I told you I was also sorry?" he whispered tantalizingly, his mouth seeking out the vulnerable place behind her ear. Lazily his hand toyed with the wing of hair in the way.

"Sorry! Sorry for what?" she challenged, wishing she

could cry but far too angry to do any such thing. She stood rigidly in his embrace, stoically ignoring the inviting gentleness of his mouth and the sensuous heat of his body. She had learned her lesson last night. Never again would she let her emotions run away with her common sense. What a fool she had been!

"For getting you involved in that stupid tavern brawl last night, for the cheap motel room, for stranding you two hours away from home in strange surroundings, for taking you out of your world and showing you something of mine. . . ."

"Beginning to realize you handled it all wrong, are you?" she flung back waspishly, closing her eyes fiercely against the tenderness in his mouth and hands. She would not let herself be seduced again!

"Yes," he admitted wryly. "I never meant to put you in a temper like this! I never meant to spend our first night together in a place like this and I never meant to wind up in a honky-tonk with you, either. But you just kept pushing. . . ."

"So now it's my fault again, is it?"

He sighed. "Why don't we call it quits and start over again? I'll take you home and we can do things right this time around. I'll go back to my Southern-gentleman accountant role and show you that I've put truck stops and barroom brawls behind me. Trust me, Dara," he added on a low, husky note. "You won't regret it. . . ."

"You're right. I won't regret it because I don't intend to let you try to repolish your image! I'll always have the memory of waking up in this place and hearing you tell me you were pleased with the transaction. Nothing will wipe that out of my mind, Yale! And I'm smart enough to know better than to cast pearls before swine twice!"

He whitened at that. She felt the sudden tension in him and knew a moment's genuine fear. Unconsciously, she touched her tongue to her lower lip, wondering if she really had gone too far this time. Eyes wide and reflecting an appeal of which she wasn't aware, Dara waited for his reaction.

"Your temper is as strong as your passion, isn't it?" he finally observed in an even tone which startled her. She knew he was exerting a considerable effort to avoid wrapping his hands around her throat. The knowledge gave her a perverse pleasure.

"You haven't seen the half of it yet," she vowed feelingly, tossing her head with scorn. "Give me an opportunity and I'll prove my temper is a lot more interesting than my passion!"

A slow smile twisted his mouth as he ran a reminiscent gaze over her face and bare shoulders. "Nothing could interest me as much as the feel of you coming alive under my hands!" he retorted gently, eyes softening. "You are all the woman a man could want, my sweet Dara. Go ahead and threaten me all you like, it won't make any difference. You're mine now."

Her eyes narrowed. "I don't belong to you or any other man. Take your hands off me, Yale. I want to go home."

He hesitated, as if considering the best method of handling her. "Maybe you'll be in a better mood after breakfast," he tried lightly, sliding his hands sensuously down her arms and catching hold of her wrists. "Shall I feed you, little tabby?" he asked whimsically, turning his head to kiss the delicate inside of her wrist. His eyes gleamed. "Will that put you in a more loving mood?"

"What do you care?" she challenged icily. "You're not interested in love. Only a business transaction!"

"I'll bet," he hazarded sadly, "that if I made an apology for that remark this morning you wouldn't accept it, would you?"

"No, I would not! Nothing you can say now will wipe out your earlier words! I know better than to trust you, Yale Ransom. I've learned my lesson!"

He drew a deep breath, and Dara knew he was still undecided about how to deal with her mood. "Well, we might as well try the food first. If that doesn't work, I'm sure I'll think of something else. Go and get dressed, honey. We'll talk this out eventually. . . ."

She tugged free of his hands, walking regally across the room to retrieve her clothes and then sweeping into the bath without a backward glance. Damn the barbarian! She would not give in to tears. Not over a man like that!

She tried vainly to plot revenge in the shower, using the washcloth savagely in an effort to remove all traces of him. The rush of water over her face made the desire to cry even stronger. But she stifled it, keeping her anger whipped up instead.

By the time she had stepped out and toweled briskly, Dara felt she had herself under control. She had sternly opted for a cold, austere manner in the hope it would help her get through the next few hours with some dignity. It was all a woman had at a time like this. Revenge was wishful thinking.

"Well, it's safe to say there won't be many women dressed like that at breakfast!" Yale quipped humorously as she stepped out of the bathroom.

She chose to ignore him, turning to the mirror to run a comb through her hair. His eyes met hers there and he smiled, trying to coax her into a better mood.

"But you do look good in green," he tried, studying the dress. He was wearing his jockey shorts now, his tanned body looking lean and powerful as he held the dark slacks and white shirt lightly clasped in one hand.

"Go to hell," she told him briefly and had the satisfaction of seeing his eyes narrow.

Without another word he stalked into the bathroom.

Twenty minutes later he ushered her into the twenty-four-hour coffee shop next door to the motel, gallantly moving to put himself between her and the curious eyes which glanced up from early-morning coffee to blink at the sight of a woman in an emerald cocktail dress. Dara made no objection as Yale seated her in a far booth and slid in beside her.

He was wearing his glasses again this morning and his sleeves were neatly buttoned at the cuff. The honey-colored hair was tidy and there was a general air of restraint about him. Dara's lips quirked downward in disgust. Nothing Yale Ransom did now would fool her. She knew the kind of man he really was.

"What would you like?" he asked politely as the waitress appeared to take their order.

"Cold cereal, please," Dara said crisply, giving her order directly to the brunette woman holding the pad and pencil. "And coffee."

"You need more than that," Yale interrupted with a frown, scanning the menu. "Bring her a number three. And the same for me."

The woman dutifully scratched Dara's order from the pad and wrote the new one. With a casual nod, she left.

"That was a waste of food and money," Dara informed him coldly. "I'm not hungry."

"You need a nice, hot breakfast," he began in a lecturing tone.

"Forget it," she gritted in resignation, lifting her eyes heavenward in silent appeal. "I'll eat it if it will stop you from talking to me as if I were a child!"

"You're not a child, you're a woman scorned, remember?" he muttered grimly. "Except that you're not exactly being scorned. But those are petty details to a female in your present frame of mind."

Dara refused to look at him, her eyes following the waitress as the woman returned to the table with coffee.

"At least she isn't staring at your outfit," Yale observed quietly when they were alone.

"She's probably been on duty since midnight. You see a little of everything sooner or later on that shift," Dara explained woodenly, sipping her coffee with care.

"How do you know?" Yale sounded mildly surprised.

"Because I've worked it." She shrugged, still refusing to glance in his direction.

"You've worked in a place like this?"

"Every summer while I was in college," she explained shortly, not particularly interested in pursuing the conversation.

"No kidding? What else have you done? I think you said something last night about only recently having become a stockbroker."

Dara favored him with a baleful gaze at that question. "Why do you want to know?"

He shrugged, lifting his coffee cup and eyeing her over the rim. "I suppose I'm kind of curious."

"Take a tip from me. Curiosity doesn't pay," she retorted flatly.

One amber brow went up. "We are singing a different tune this morning, aren't we?"

Dara gritted her teeth, about to dredge up a scathing reply when a deep, cheerfully rumbling male voice interrupted the conversation.

"Excuse me, folks, but the little lady in green wouldn't happen to be a stockbroker by any chance, would she?"

Dara glanced up, startled, to find a huge, friendly-looking man in his mid-forties staring down at her with smiling gray eyes. He reminded her a lot of Hank Bonner in his choice of a size thirty-four belt for a waistline considerably larger. The man was dressed in a plaid flannel shirt and faded jeans. He had long-distance trucker written all over him.

"May I ask who wants to know?" Yale's question was polite, but there was a firmness to it that drew the man's respectful attention.

"Sam's the name. Sam Tyler," he said at once, extending a wide paw of a hand to shake Yale's. "And I'll bet your name's Ransom, right?"

"You seem to know a good deal more about us than

71

we know about you," Yale pointed out with a deliberate smile.

"There couldn't be two ladies in green at this particular truck stop on this particular morning. Mind if I join you for a cup? Hank Bonner's the source of my information, by the way."

"I see," Yale said slowly, speculatively. "Sit down, by all means. Where did you run into Hank?"

"Having coffee a ways down the line. He knew I was headin' north and asked me to deliver a message if I found you two at this café. Also suggested you might be needing a ride into Eugene!"

"That was thoughtful of him," Dara said quickly, wondering why Yale seemed a little aloof. She had been wondering how they were going to get home.

"He also said to tell you the hand was doing fine," Sam added with a smile.

"I'm glad. What was the message?" Dara asked encouragingly. Yale seemed a little more relaxed now.

"Well, I guess I'd have to say that's a tad more serious. . . ." The big trucker's gaze sobered and he turned to face Yale.

"Trouble?" Yale's eyes were cool and more alert than the situation seemed to call for, Dara decided.

"A little, I reckon. Hank said he mentioned his, uh, special cargo to you?"

"He did," Yale said briefly, ignoring Dara's frown.

She glanced from one man to the other, perplexed. "What are you talking about? What 'special cargo'?"

A silent look passed between the two men. The sort of Do-we-tell-the-little-lady-about-this-or-not? glance that was enough to boil a woman's blood. And Dara was already on a high simmer.

Yale considered the relentless expression in the gray-green ice of her eyes and appeared to come to a reluctant decision.

"A short while before we met Hank last night he stumbled across something unexpected being shipped in his truck. Something which had been taped to the cab in an inconspicuous place by someone who apparently intended to retrieve it later. Probably after Hank had obligingly brought it down from Canada and across a couple of state lines. . . ."

"What sort of 'something'? Drugs?"

"She's right quick, ain't she?" Sam Tyler offered admiringly to Yale as if complimenting him on a well-trained horse.

"A little too quick at times, I'm afraid," Yale growled, shooting Dara a withering glance. "At any rate, Hank removed the stuff and then put out a quiet warning to friends at a few stops. They didn't spill it on the CB because he had hopes of catching the guy when he came looking for his stuff."

"Why didn't Hank go straight to the police with it when he found it?" Dara demanded, brows drawing together across her nose.

Once again Yale and Sam traded glances, and Yale finally said quietly, "There were reasons. Besides, it was just a small, er, personal amount. . . ."

"We all figure it's a one-man maneuver. It's been done before," Sam tossed in helpfully. "The logical place for the pickup is somewhere south of the California-Oregon border. . . ."

"After it's been driven across the state line," Dara put in.

"Right. But it didn't happen that way. The guy came for his pickup at the first stop Hank hit after letting you two off. Even though they weren't really expecting him that soon, Hank and a friend damned near caught him." Sam hesitated. "They did get a description of him which, after what you might call due consideration"—he grinned—"they turned over to the police. The sonova—

pardon me, ma'am—the joker's got both the cops and half the folks on the Interstate watching for him now. Sooner or later he'll turn up."

"The situation seems to be under control," Yale murmured, clearly waiting for a punch line. Sam delivered it.

"Hank's pretty sure the guy will be picked up soon. Which will be a great relief to all concerned, naturally. . . ."

"Naturally." Yale grinned, and once again Dara had the feeling she wasn't being told everything.

"But it occurred to him that if this, uh, joker's monitoring the CB jabber it might explain why he came for his stuff before it crossed the border. . . ." Sam let the sentence trail off suggestively.

"Damn CB gossip!" Yale muttered.

"Okay, guys," Dara began vengefully. "Let's not lose the 'quick' one in the crowd just as she's beginning to catch up! What's the real problem? Why is Hank sending messages back to us?"

Sam looked at Yale and lifted a huge shoulder. Yale nodded and turned to Dara.

"Shortly after he let us off last night, at the very next stop, in fact, someone came looking for the 'cargo'. . . ."

"And . . . ?" It was like pulling teeth, she decided grimly, but her pride wasn't going to get in the way of her overriding curiosity. Dara was determined to get all the answers.

"By then the shipment had been removed," Yale went on gently.

"Obviously! You said Hank removed it at once!"

"And you and I constitute the main alteration in Hank's normal routine on the Interstate through Oregon. Whoever taped that stuff on the truck wouldn't have had much trouble learning that Hank had given a lift to a couple of strangers. He might have come to check that the cargo was still in place after the hitchhikers got off.

Finding it gone, a disinterested observer might be excused for wondering if the cargo had gotten off with us."

"Oh," Dara muttered weakly as the light dawned. "The guy might think we hijacked his drugs?"

"A perverted thinker who didn't know our sterling characters might have come to that conclusion, yes," Yale said patiently. "Eat your eggs, they're getting cold."

"I'm not hungry," Dara said absently, her mind churning with the unexpected news. "You mean that creep might come after us?"

"A lot of folks heard about you on the air last night," Sam put in kindly. "Frankly, we don't figure it's very likely the guy will bother chasing you down. In the first place, the cargo wasn't that, er, large. And in the second place, if he's still listening to the CB he knows he's being hunted. If he's got any sense he'll fade into the sunset."

"I'll keep an eye on her until we know for sure the guy's been found," Yale announced casually, digging into his sausage.

"I'll keep an eye on myself," Dara snapped, and then another thought struck her. "Do the police know we were with Hank last night, Sam?"

"Don't believe he saw any point in mentioning you two," Sam assured her smilingly.

"Good!" Dara heaved a sigh of relief. A lot of people knew she'd left that party in the company of Yale Ransom. A lot of other people knew she'd been out joyriding on the Interstate and had wound up at a cheap truck-stop motel. If somehow the first group found out what the second group knew via a newspaper story . . . She winced. It didn't bear thinking about. Eugene was a small town and she wasn't sure how much a stockbroker's reputation could stand. Or an accountant's, for that matter! People didn't like trusting their hard-earned money to wild and reckless types!

As if he'd been following her thoughts, Yale smiled cryptically.

"Worrying about your reputation, or mine?"

"You take care of yourself and I'll look after myself!" she told him morosely.

Something wicked glinted in the hazel eyes behind the lenses of Yale's glasses. "The police haven't been told about us, but an enterprising newsperson looking to beef up a tale of interstate smuggling might do a little more research than is absolutely necessary."

Dara stared at him, stricken.

"Eat your breakfast, honey," Yale growled, appearing almost contrite at having added to her fears.

"I think I'm going to be sick," she informed him grandly.

5

~~~~~~~~~~~~~~~~~~~~

Are you going to sulk for the rest of the weekend?" Yale inquired with apparently detached interest as he opened the door of the Alfa Romeo two hours later and stuffed Dara inside.

"Why do you care? I'm not going to be spending the weekend with you anyway!"

He slammed the door shut with a narrow-eyed glance and walked around the hood. In the distance Sam Tyler's truck lumbered up the empty street in search of the Interstate entrance. In a short while Dara would be home. She was extraordinarily grateful for the knowledge.

"How long do you usually stay in this sort of mood?" Yale asked as he slid behind the wheel.

"Shut up and take me home."

"I can't. I don't know where you live."

Gritting her teeth, Dara gave him directions. As he pulled away from the curb she glanced back down the street at the now silent bar. As long as she lived in Eugene it was going to remain the landmark of her debacle, she decided sadly.

"I just wish Hank had gone to the cops before we ran into him." She sighed. "And if that wish could be granted, I'd go on to wish that we'd never run into Hank!"

"Don't blame him for what happened last night. That was strictly between you and me," Yale growled, guiding the car through the quiet morning.

"But why did he wait until the guy came looking for the stuff before going to the cops?" she persisted. That point bothered her.

"It wouldn't have been convenient for Hank to go to the police at the time he found the extra cargo," Yale said patiently.

"Why not?"

"Your curiosity is beginning to return, isn't it?" he noted in a cheerier tone.

"As you have already pointed out, I'm not in the best of moods this morning. Are you going to answer me or not?"

Yale sighed. "Hank wasn't anxious to drag the cops into this because he was carrying a hot load."

"What?" Dara swung around to stare at him in astonishment. "Hank was carrying stolen goods?"

"No, 'hot goods' means that he was just carrying an unauthorized load. Trucking regulations specify what kinds of goods drivers are allowed to transport. Hank was hoping he could take care of the guy himself and that would be the end of it. But when he and his pal missed snagging the man last night they decided it would be better to haul in the cops. So Hank probably got rid of his cargo—which, incidentally, was a shipment of T.V. sets—and then went to the police with his story."

"You and he certainly got chummy up there in the front seat while I was dozing in that sleeper!"

"We had . . . things in common, I suppose you'd say," Yale admitted.

"How much in common?" Dara glanced at him suspiciously. "Don't tell me you try to take the law into your own hands, too? Not a proper, upstanding accountant like you!" She didn't bother to keep the scathing tone out of her last words.

"No," he said, a strange smile coming easily to the hard mouth. A reminiscent sort of smile. "But I know what it's like to avoid the police. Remember, there are a lot of illegal stills up in those blue hills where I come from."

"Illegal stills?" Dara drew in her breath as realization dawned. "Yale! You didn't! You weren't a . . . a . . ." She broke off, suddenly enthralled. "How *did* you work your way through college?" she demanded.

He flicked her a derisive glance and then brought his attention back to his driving. "I did what paid the most," he told her laconically.

"You ran moonshine? Illegal whiskey?" She was fascinated.

He nodded once, not looking at her.

"They still do that back there?" she pressed, intrigued.

"The business is bigger than ever. The Feds will never kill it. You folks on the Coast have your million-dollar drug busts, and back in the hill country we had our million-dollar illegal liquor busts."

"It seems different somehow, though. I mean, I've never really thought of moonshine whiskey as being in the same category as imported drugs like heroin."

"You don't think white lightning's taken its share of victims?" he asked coolly. "It's a hell of a lot more dangerous than a lot of drugs!"

"Well, I suppose it's as dangerous as any alcohol . . ." she agreed slowly.

"Alcoholism isn't the only problem associated with it,"

Yale snapped. "Anyone buying it runs the same risk of getting contaminated stuff as someone scoring any other drug on the street. Some of it really will cause blindness. Not to mention the possibility of lead poisoning. There are a lot of 'shine addicts back in the states around the Appalachian Mountains."

"One thinks of it as a kind of folk tradition or something," Dara said, lifting a hand in a small, helpless gesture.

"Oh, it's a tradition, all right," Yale conceded bitterly. "Passed down from father to son. The kids grow up in families where being an adult male means being able to drink the stuff. They can't wait. And it goes on from one generation to the next."

"And the women?" she asked softly, curiously.

"They have to live with the men who are addicted. Most of the violence the stuff produces comes out in the home. You can use your imagination."

Dara sat silently for a moment, thinking of the memories she had stirred awake in Yale's mind by her rashness the previous evening.

"Did you know how bad the stuff was when you were running it?" she asked tentatively.

He just threw her a pitying glance. "Do I look like the naive type?"

"Er, no."

"It was the only game in town when I was growing up. About the only viable industry in the area. It sure as hell was where the money was at, and I knew from the start I was going to need two things to get out of those mountains: money and an education. I needed the first to buy the second."

"And you got it." It was a statement of fact.

"I got part of the education and then I got married to a high-school acquaintance who saw me as her ticket out of the mountains." His mouth twisted with astonishing bitterness. Dara felt a cold chill down her spine.

"Then what happened?" She knew she ought to stop asking questions, but something drove her on, demanding to know the whole story.

"Then I needed more money and a more legal way to get it." Yale shrugged. "I got a job driving trucks for a couple of years. It worked. We got out of the mountains."

"And . . . ?"

He slanted a glance across the seat, taking in Dara's intent expression. "And she found someone who could take her farther than just out of the mountains."

"She left you?"

"Yes. Best for all concerned, as it turned out," he went on with a philosophical inflection. "She married someone who could give her a lot more than I could, and I had another chance to go back to school. Which I did."

"Emerging a proper, dignified accountant at last, hmm?" Dara smiled, relaxing finally now that she had the whole story.

"Satisfied?" he asked sardonically.

"Just think," she retorted, "if you'd given me all those answers last night we would never have wound up in that awful situation!"

"So it's all my fault again?"

"It's been your fault from the beginning!"

"The argument is academic at this point," he told her evenly, slowing as they approached the street on which her apartment was located. A jogger passed the Alfa Romeo, headed in the opposite direction along one of the many paths the town had established for cyclists and joggers.

"Meaning?" she challenged.

"Meaning you're mine. Regardless of how it all happened, the ultimate result is the same."

"Damn it! Don't talk like that!" she suddenly yelped as he parked the car in front of her apartment.

"Like what?" Yale asked innocently, turning in the seat to face her.

"As if . . . as if you own me or something because of what happened last nght!" Her temporary satisfaction at having her questions about him answered evaporated in the presence of his continued threat.

"But I do," he explained gently, hazel eyes gleaming. He moved, uncoiling with astonishing speed to forestall her effort to dive out of the car.

"Don't run away from me, honey," he soothed, his hand manacling her wrist with a grip that would only hurt if she struggled too hard. "I've told you I'm sorry about the way everything happened. It wasn't the hearts and flowers and romance you deserve, I admit that. Let me show you I can do better than a truck-stop motel. . . ."

"You're out of your head if you think I'm going to let you hang around for . . . for more of what happened last night!" Dara gasped, appalled at the intensity in him. Dear God in heaven! Why did he have to look so *sincere*? But maybe he *was* sincere, she corrected herself grimly. Maybe he had decided he was in the market for an affair and she had practically invited him into one!

"Last night was good and you know it," he told her firmly, voice deepening with husky meaning. "Stop fighting it, Dara. It's happened and we're involved now. Nothing's going to change that."

"The hell it isn't! You may have decided you're content with the 'transaction,' but I've had a lot of second and third thoughts! I'm withdrawing from the bargain. Give your damn account to someone else!"

"I apologize for that remark . . ." he began, his fingers tightening on her wrist. "Let me explain!"

"Explain! Explain that you're accustomed to bargaining for . . . for love? I don't want to hear your explanations!"

"Love?" he questioned softly, mouth curving. "Was that what I was going to get out of the deal? Your love?"

"You'll never know, will you?" she charged violently, horribly afraid he might feel the trembling anger and pain in her. Desperately she tried to keep her voice cold and callous. "Because the deal is off!"

"How can it be when it was so perfectly consummated?" he murmured, pulling her forward until she fell lightly against his chest. "And you are quite perfect, you know," he went on whimsically, ignoring her struggles while he used his free hand to smooth the curve of her hair. His finger trailed from the burnt-russet wave to the edge of her angry mouth.

"Can't you at least try to resurrect some of those fine Southern manners you were showing off last night before you reverted to a . . . a trucker?" she managed breathlessly, aware of the heat and strength of him as he held her close. "I don't like being mauled on a Saturday morning in front of the entire neighborhood!"

"It wasn't my fine Southern manners you wanted last night," he reminded her, bending his head down until the hard mouth hovered an inch above her lips. "What you got was the real me, and don't try telling me you didn't like it. You were all softness and warmth and sweet, feminine demand in my arms last night. I'll never forget it, honey, even if the surroundings weren't what they should have been for the occasion. . . ."

"No!" But the protest was issued as a small squeak of dismay which died beneath the onslaught of Yale's kiss.

Almost instantly, it seemed, his caress re-created the seductive aura of the dream-filled state in which he had made love to her last night. His mouth was firm and moved invitingly, coaxingly on hers. She heard his stifled groan of need as he urged her lips apart with his tongue, and when her mouth opened to him of its own volition her senses were throbbing.

It was hopeless, Dara thought dazedly. In his arms, she was too vulnerable and her love was far too exposed. Did he know the effect he had on her? How she longed to unbutton his shirt and lace her fingers through the amber hair of his chest? How her body pulsed with memories of the pleasure it had known last night and with the need to satisfy the man who had given rise to that strange pleasure? Did he know how very much in love she was?

When at last he lifted his head to smile crookedly down into her bemused eyes, Dara wanted to beg him to continue his lovemaking. She knew beyond a shadow of a doubt he was reading her state of mind in her wide, gray-geen gaze. The crooked smile broadened.

"I'll take you out to dinner tonight," he promised caressingly, his hand stroking the length of her back to the base of her spine. "We'll do it properly this time, I swear. . . ."

"That's . . . that's impossible," she finally got out with some semblance of haughtiness. She was not going to let this man treat her so shabbily again! Regardless of what her heart was willing to forgive, her mind still functioned and was in control! "I have a date this evening."

"Break it," he ordered gently.

"Why should I? His account might be even larger than yours!" That hadn't been particularly wise, but Dara was feeling driven. Nevertheless, as his hands tightened with sudden warning on her, she wished she'd found another insult.

"Dara, you ought to have learned something from last night," Yale growled thickly. "If nothing else, you should know by now that it's not wise to push me too far. Either break your date for this evening or take the consequences!"

"What consequences?"

"Honey, if you flaunt someone else in my face now that you're mine, I swear I'll take him apart," he gritted in such a flat, deadly voice she believed him.

"Another example of your good manners?" she scoffed, trying to hide her shock. "Is this the kind of behavior I can expect now that you've announced your intention to treat me as I deserve?"

The amber lashes flickered closed for an instant and Dara could feel Yale putting a rein on his temper. It was more than a little unnerving to be so close to the source of a potential explosion. When he opened his eyes again, the lenses of the horn-rimmed glasses couldn't hide the degree of control he was exercising.

"I'm doing my best to be patient with you, Dara," he said stiffly. "I know you've been through a lot in the past several hours. Much more than you bargained for. . . ."

"You can say that again! I wasn't even planning on transacting business when I went to that party last night. Goes to show how life is just full of little surprises!"

"You know, I could cheerfully take a belt to you this morning!"

"Really? Is that how you treat your women?"

"You seem bent on finding out for yourself!" he rasped, shaking his head in quick exasperation. "And if you aren't waiting very meekly at the door for me this evening, I may treat you to a firsthand demonstration of my techniques! In you go, Dara. I'll pick you up at six. And don't wear your jeans. We're not going to any of your favorite nightclubs!"

Several hours later, after a lot of furious heart-searching and grim lectures to herself, Dara paced the floor of her apartment, for all the world like a restless cat. A tabby cat. She knew she was waiting for the sophisticated roar of the Alfa Romeo.

She couldn't deny it, she thought gloomily. She was in love. She had fallen in love last night, and nothing was going to change that fact very quickly. She was a woman who prided herself on a pragmatic approach to life. She would deal with the reality of the situation and not pretend she was merely temporarily infatuated. She knew what infatuation was. It was what she had felt for her ex-husband. And now she knew what love was.

There were cures for being in love, just as there were

cures for infatuation, she told herself firmly. But the
remedies for love were likely to have some severe side
effects. And they didn't work quickly, as far as she knew.
Time was one of them. Time and throwing oneself into
work and perhaps finding another man . . . She would
try them all. As soon as she could free herself from Yale
Ransom!

Chewing absently on her lower lip, she came to a brief
halt in front of a hall mirror and ran a quick, assessing eye
over herself. There had been no date to cancel for this
evening. Jeff Conroy, the research analyst from the
office, was out of town on business and she hadn't felt
like seeing any of her other assorted escorts. She almost
hadn't gone to her manager's party last night, in fact. Too
bad she hadn't followed her inclinations!

The curving bell of her deep red hair was brushed and
polished-looking in the glow of the lamp. The floating
material of the exotically printed yellow and green dress
fell flatteringly over her rounded breasts and softly flaring
hips. She had chosen her highest-heeled sandals in an
effort to be on more equal footing with Yale, but she was
very much afraid that wouldn't be a lot of help. He
tended to dominate everyone in his vicinity.

On the whole, she had to be reasonably satisfied with
the overall effect. She looked poised, cool and very much
in command of herself. It was as much as she could hope
for under the circumstances, she thought with a sigh as
the sound of a car stopping out front caught her attention.

She opened the door to find Yale standing on the step,
every inch the neat, conservatively dressed professional.
For some reason she almost laughed, barely managing to
stifle the flash of humor. But he must have seen it in her
eyes, because the gold winked in his grin and the hazel
eyes glittered wickedly behind the austere glasses.

"Why do you have to look past the surface?" he

complained, stepping inside the cozy apartment and glancing around expectantly. "I really am an accountant, you know. Give me a chance!" He finished his quick perusal of the room and lifted her chin possessively with his hand. Dropping a light, proprietary kiss on her lips, he released her almost at once.

"I gave you a chance," she reminded him determinedly. "And you turned out to be something altogether different than an accountant!" She moved away from him. "I'll get my purse."

She disappeared into the bedroom and returned to find him studying her eclectic collection of books. He put down the small volume of eighteenth-century philosophy as she appeared in the doorway.

"Your interests appear to be wide-ranging," he murmured, coming forward. "Do you play that guitar?" He nodded toward the instrument on the wall.

"A little," she admitted carefully, eyeing him uneasily.

"And can you really cook stuff out of those fancy gourmet cookbooks?"

"Do I look like I've been starving to death most of my life?" she tossed back, reaching for a fluffy shawl.

He came up behind her, adjusting the shawl and then sliding his hands warmly down her sides, shaping her curves. "No," he whispered throatily. "You look like a woman who knows instinctively about womanly things like cooking and loving and—"

"And selling securities!" she interrupted, stepping hastily away from his touch.

"And selling securities," he agreed, smiling. He flicked a glance over her interestedly. "Tonight's my night to ask the questions," he went on slowly.

"I thought you were going to take a lesson from me in the perils of curiosity," she muttered, turning briskly toward the door.

"I won't complain if my curiosity leads us to bed as

yours did last night." He chuckled, following her out the door and into the dusk of the spring evening.

"It won't!" she swore. "Nothing will lead me into a repeat of last night! Unlike you, I've learned my lesson!"

"What did he say?" Yale asked almost conversationally as he helped her into the car and took his place behind the wheel.

"Who?" She frowned, momentarily at a loss.

"The guy you broke the date with tonight."

"That's none of your business," she declared regally, glancing pointedly out the window.

"Everything about you is my business now," he told her patiently. "But I'll let that question ride. After all, you didn't try to force a confrontation. I'll be satisfied with that."

"You're too generous!"

"I know, but that's probably because I'm feeling guilty."

"Over last night?" she scoffed. "I don't believe you."

"Try me. Give me a chance, honey. I'll make everything right this time around."

She slanted a suspicious glance across the seat, not certain how to react. This sudden earnestness to start over left her confused and wary.

"Tell me about yourself," he ordered in a rather businesslike fashion some time later as they were seated in a charming downtown restaurant. One of the new Oregon-grown and -bottled wines was on the table, the atmosphere was elegantly subdued and the other patrons were well dressed and well mannered. Yale had brought her a long way from last night, Dara thought with fleeting humor.

"What do you want to know?" she asked, picking up the menu with a sense of anticipation. The food really was very good here, and Dara appreciated good food.

He shrugged. "Anything. Everything. Are you a native?"

88

"Native Oregonian? Definitely," she informed him, scanning the list of Continental specialties.

"Have you ever been outside the state?" he asked in amusement.

"Only when absolutely necessary," she told him with the blissful smugness of the classic Oregonian. "I was forced to go to California once for a time and I've made a couple of brief forays into Washington." She shuddered in recollection.

"I'm beginning to feel that way myself, and I've only been here a short while," Yale chuckled.

She glanced up and met his laughing eyes. "Most new immigrants want to be the last ones allowed over the border. They'd like to see the place closed off once they're safely here. You know, issue passports and visas to the rest of the folks who want to come for a visit!"

"You can't blame us," he said gently, watching her face with deep interest. "Oregon is so unspoiled and has so much to offer. We newcomers feel like we've found a paradise, and we know how easily paradises are ruined. What amazes me is that you natives are equally conscious of what you've got."

She nodded, perfectly aware of what he was talking about. "We've got everything that counts. The outdoors is everywhere, even in the cities. We're proud of our past and we've preserved it. We're very self-reliant, a heritage from that past, I suppose. A lot of us are descendants of people who came out west on wagon trains, you know. Our towns and cities are manageable in size. Portland's our only 'big' city, and that's only about four hundred thousand people. A lot of people make their living in the lumber industry, and that tends to breed an independent spirit."

"Everything about this state is independent," Yale murmured, trying his wine tentatively. It was his first exposure to Oregon wines. "Your environmentalist attitudes are famous throughout the rest of the nation, you know. You're all considered flaming radicals on the East Coast! Your state and local governments have spent a fortune taking care of your rivers and air and land."

"We know what we've got." She shrugged. "Land this beautiful doesn't last unless it's taken care of."

He nodded. "I'm aware of that."

"Why did you move from California?" Dara asked.

"L.A. turned out to be a little too far from the hills," Yale confided with surprising honesty.

Dara's lashes flicked against her high cheekbones as she considered that. "So you came looking for someplace a little more real, is that it?"

"Something like that," he agreed reflectively. "I don't ever want to go back to the mountains, but I found out I didn't want to give up everything I'd taken for granted as a child, either. I like smaller towns. I'll never be at home in a huge metropolis. And I like having the outdoors in my backyard."

"You can take the boy out of the country, but you can't take the country out of the boy?" Dara grinned in sudden sympathy.

"I guess that's it," he said slowly, returning her smile.

In that moment of communication Dara realized she had made a huge mistake. She had unwittingly allowed him to establish the truce he had been seeking.

"And that, my darling Dara," Yale continued, cementing the truce with sure instinct, "is something I hadn't even admitted to myself until you forced the realization on me. You're a witch, sweetheart."

"Do people back in the mountains still believe in witches?" she whispered, aware of the sensual tension she was experiencing.

"Definitely. Just because we talk a little slower than the rest of you doesn't mean we think any slower!"

He danced with her after dinner. Not in the restrained way he had danced at the flashy, ex-disco nightclub nor in the earthy, blatantly sexual way he had at the truckers' bar. This time Yale held her close, the embrace intimate but not embarrassing, and Dara foolishly allowed herself to revel in the swaying, enticing strength of his lean body.

She knew she was being seduced; knew it and for the life of her didn't know how to combat it. She loved this man in all his complexity, and saying no to him tonight was going to take more willpower than she might have in reserve. But it must be said. Her whole future depended on it.

6

~~~~~~~~~~~~~~~

As much as she had tried to prepare herself for the inevitable difficulty of ending the evening adroitly, and even with all her considerable experience at ending such evenings with other men, Dara had to acknowledge later that she badly mishandled the event. She found herself detonating the male time bomb in her hands with hardly any effort at all.

"I hope you're going to invite me to stay the night," Yale said deliberately, setting aside the guitar on which he'd picked out a couple of haunting mountain melodies for her and reaching for the glass of brandy Dara had poured.

So matter-of-fact! Dara drew a deep breath and said very carefully, "No, Yale. Not tonight." She sat quite still and watchful on her end of the couch and waited.

"Tonight, especially," he contradicted quietly, his eyes meeting hers with cool certainty.

In spite of herself, Dara shivered. "Why do you say that?" she whispered.

"Because I'm supposed to be keeping an eye on you, remember?" Yale allowed himself a smile at her look of astonishment.

Dara arched an eyebrow quellingly. "To tell you the truth, I'd almost forgotten about that small-time smuggler. But it doesn't matter. We both know he's not likely to show up. He doesn't even know our names."

"He could have followed us this morning, waiting until tonight to come calling," Yale suggested helpfully.

"Don't be ridiculous! You're making excuses and you know it!"

"You're right." He sighed. "I really don't need any other excuse than the obvious, do I?"

"You're not staying here tonight, Yale. The evening has been lovely, I'll admit that much, but not lovely enough to cause me to make a fool out of myself again. This is as far as you're going to get with your seduction."

He considered that for a moment. "I'm going to stay," he announced flatly.

"Then you'll have to sleep outside in the Alfa Romeo, because you most certainly aren't staying here. Good night, Yale." With an air of determination, Dara rose to her feet.

He leaned back into the corner of the couch, one leg stretched out along the cushions with the foot dangling. The picture of the relaxed male, she thought in dismay. His dark tie had been loosened and his jacket lay over the back of the couch. Some of the rakishness of last night was back. It set off all the alarms Yale had spent the evening silencing.

"Yale," she tried reasonably, "what happened last night was bad enough, but only a bunch of truckers whom we'll never see again know about it. If you stay here tonight all my neighbors will know! As you yourself pointed out, this isn't Los Angeles! If you're not concerned about my reputation, you ought to think about your own."

He sipped his brandy and contemplated the unicorn tapestry on the far wall. "An interesting notion." He turned his head to look at her speculatively. "It occurs to me that I *am* the injured party in all this. It was my reputation you set about tearing down last night. . . ."

"Don't be an idiot! All I ever did was ask you a few questions! You're the one who—"

"Let's not get into that argument again. We're never going to agree on whose fault it was that we wound up at that motel last night." He groaned good-naturedly, wriggling his shoe a couple of times as he stared at the tip. "But I am staying, sweetheart. I'm a little concerned about that creep still being on the loose. I won't be comfortable thinking about you alone here."

"Yale . . . !" Dara opened her mouth in mounting frustration.

"I won't force myself on you, for God's sake," he told her irritably. "I'll sleep out here on the couch."

"That's not going to help the problem of my reputation!"

"Or mine. But I suppose we'll live it down," he said philosophically.

For some reason his nonchalance was the match to her kindling.

"Why you . . . you *bastard!* How dare you spend the evening behaving so perfectly when all along you were planning this! If you think I'm going to tolerate . . . oh!"

Her eyes blazed up at him as he leaped to his feet, all the lazy gentleness vanishing instantly.

"That's enough! You've called me a bastard twice today, and that's twice too often!" Yale had his hands on her shoulders before Dara could slip aside. The hazel eyes echoed her own simmering fury, and Dara was acutely aware of the fact that he had far more strength than she had to back his anger.

"I told myself I was going to be patient with you, give

94

you a chance to cool off after this morning, but maybe the temper I saw then is routine for you! If that's the case, then I'm going to have to do something about it. Beginning now!" He gave her a small, decisive shake. "Apologize, Dara! There was a time when I would have taken a knife to any man who called me a name like that!"

"Why don't you try that approach?" she bit out recklessly. "You probably still carry one in your sock for old times' sake!"

"There are other tactics one can use on a woman," he warned silkily, forcing her closer.

"Don't you dare threaten me, Yale Ransom!"

"How are you going to stop me, Dara Bancroft?" he said with a hint of savagery. One hand sliding up to grip her nape and hold her steady as if she were a kitten, Yale snapped off his glasses and tossed them down onto the circular glass coffee table. Then his hand went to his loosened tie, pulling it free. It followed the glasses. His eyes never left her frozen face as his fingers went to the top button of his shirt.

"Stop it, Yale! I mean it, damn you!"

"I want an apology, Dara. A heartfelt one, I think."

"Why should I apologize?" she managed bravely. "It's the truth."

"I know. Which is probably why I want the apology," he retorted, his fingers on the second button of his shirt.

"You know?" she repeated in blank confusion.

"Umm. My father was killed in a fight before he got around to marrying my mother."

"Oh! Yale, Yale!" Dara lifted her palms to his face, her heart in her eyes. "You must know I never meant it literally! It's always been just another swear word to me. Please accept my apology."

His hand stilled and he regarded her solemnly for a moment while she waited contritely for him to tell her everything was all right again. Dara could have bitten her tongue out for having fought so unfairly. The gray and green eyes were full of her anxiety as she gazed up into his face, her hands still gently framing his hard jaw.

"How can I refuse?" he whispered a little hoarsely, his fingers gliding up her arm to capture one of her hands. "When you say it so nicely." He touched his lips to the sensitive area of her palm, first kissing it and then closing his teeth ever so tantalizingly on the flesh at the base of her thumb. The utter eroticism of the caress chilled her.

"Yale?" The question in her voice was clear and tremulous. He smiled gently down into her face. Without a word he drew her against him and kissed her.

"Do you always go from raging inferno to sweetly yielding female so quickly?" he breathed in amusement as his lips feathered across hers. "I find it fascinating, you know. So much fire and so much warmth."

"Yale, no!" Dara's voice was a plea as her eyes closed involuntarily against the force of her own passion. "I won't let you stay tonight. I can't!"

"We'll talk about it in the morning," he promised thickly. She knew he was letting the arousal he had held in check all evening begin to take command. She could feel it in the growing tautness of his thighs as he used his hand to force her close against him.

"Don't fight me, honey," he begged, shifting his leg so that it thrust between hers. Off balance and terribly aware of her vulnerability in the intimate position, Dara tried to resist.

"I won't let you do it!" she whispered, pushing at him even as her body longed for the embrace. "I won't conduct another . . . another business *transaction* with you, damn it!"

"No?" he mocked huskily, his hands moving down her sides, sliding across the high breasts with loving slowness before descending to the shape of her waist. He urged her closer so that his upper thigh pressed heavily against her. The thin fabric of her dress was little protection and Dara was fully conscious of the hard maleness of him.

The undeniable evidence of his physical response to her was a seduction in itself, she realized, alarmed. She felt the rush of longing she had known the night before and began to panic.

"No!" she gasped in answer to his mocking question. "No, I will not allow another business deal between us, because you *couldn't afford the price* this time!"

The defiant words seemed to scorch the air around them. Dara froze as she felt the savage tension in him. His hands clenched into her soft flesh and his words came back angry and raw.

"What price, Dara? *Name it!* We'll find out whether or not I'll pay it!"

She was committed, forced to follow through on her wild threat. She felt backed into a corner and she came out fighting for her very survival.

"The price is marriage, Yale! I don't want you to get the idea I'm still selling myself for anything so paltry as a stock account! You'll have to marry me this time!"

A taunting wickedness flashed in the hazel eyes. "Is that your idea of revenge, little tabby?" he drawled.

"That's my idea of how to stop a Southern gentleman in his tracks!" she flung back, incensed at his barely masked humor. "Force yourself on me tonight and I will demand that you do the *honorable* thing!"

"I think," he informed her gravely, "that you're in the wrong part of the South. Where I come from we called that sort of thing a shotgun wedding. Have you got a shotgun?" he asked interestedly.

"Push me too far tonight and you'll find out!" A thoroughly ridiculous promise, Dara thought gloomily. How could you force a man to marry you? Unless, of course, his own code of honor required it. . . .

"I do believe you're trying to threaten me, sweetheart," Yale murmured, gliding his hands down her back and capturing her hips in a kneading grip. His lips hovered in the vicinity of her ear and she trembled at the overpowering nearness of him.

"Those are my terms, Yale," she breathed, her face buried in the material of his shirt as she waited with agonized suspense for the results of her reckless play. Nothing should have been more guaranteed to stop his seduction routine than the knowledge that she would be expecting marriage! Dara was certain of her weapon. The only thing she wasn't certain of was whether or not she had really wanted to use it. Another night with Yale Ransom was a temptation beyond any she had ever experienced.

"I'm amazed you think so highly of my sense of honor," he observed coolly, dropping a feather-light kiss on her temple.

Dara gave a small start of surprise. "There's no doubt in my mind that you're a man who likes to stay on even terms with the world," she gritted. "You seem to have a pay-as-you-go philosophy about life. You proved that this morning!"

"When I told you you could have my account?" He groaned and then kissed her throat just below her ear. "You may be right."

"And you're not a fool . . ." she went on carefully, wishing her body didn't react so strongly to a man she had known such a short time.

"That's a more debatable point."

"Not foolish enough to commit yourself to marriage with a woman you've only known a little over twenty-four hours!" she declared, bitter triumph lacing her words.

"I'll admit the price you're setting on yourself tonight is a bit steep," he hedged, his mouth traveling down to the curve of her shoulder.

"And I'm going to stick to it. I won't sell myself as

cheaply as you seem to think I did last night!" she cried wretchedly.

"If that's the way you want it," he said slowly, and she thought she felt him tense. He was going to leave. She knew it. Knew it and wanted insanely to call back her words.

But it was too late. She had made her decision and she would force herself to abide by it. There was the future to think about tonight, not just a few tempting hours of ecstasy with a man who considered love a business transaction!

"As long as we understand each other," he whispered thickly, "we might as well get on with the transaction."

He moved, sweeping her up into his arms with a smooth power that took away her breath.

"Yale! What are you doing?" she gasped as he started down the short hall to her bedroom. "Put me down!"

"Why? You set the terms. Don't tell me you're going to try to back out of them now."

"That's right!" she rasped furiously. "I set the terms. And I'm going to make you stick to them! I swear it!"

"Okay," he said simply, using a large foot to open the door to her darkened bedroom.

"What do you mean, 'okay'?" she yelped, the combination of passion and anger heating her veins until she felt liquid fire running through her body.

"I accept the terms," he explained evenly, dropping her lightly onto the old-fashioned country-patterned quilt that covered the four-poster bed.

She stared up at him, trying to make out his expression in the dimly lit room. She was curled in a shaft of light which fell onto the bed from the hall and she felt extraordinarily vulnerable. Everything was going wrong. She had been so sure her demand would send him fleeing into the night!

"You can't be serious!" she tried, her eyes fastened on

him in utter fascination. "Do you know what you're saying?"

Even though he stood in the shadows, Dara couldn't miss the flash of gold in his slow, sardonic grin. "Don't worry about me," he advised, stripping off his shirt and letting it fall, unheeded, to the carpet. "You should be asking yourself that question. Between last night and tonight you're going to find yourself with both me and my account to handle. And we're both going to take a lot of time and attention."

Dara scrambled to her knees on the bed, not knowing whether to lash out at him or open her arms to receive him. Was he mad? She wasn't the sort of woman who drove men to rash extremes! She hadn't even been able to seduce her ex-husband away from thoughts of his former fiancée!

Dara put out a hand in uncertain appeal as Yale began efficient work on his belt buckle.

"Yale, listen to me. You're not talking about a . . . a short fling with a woman you happened to meet at a party! You're standing there, telling me you're going to marry me! In the morning you're going to have all sorts of regrets, call yourself a fool! Don't you understand?"

"After what we found between us last night, I don't see any reason why I should have regrets," he countered, stepping out of the rest of his clothes as if he were accustomed to undressing in her bedroom. Or as if he expected to become accustomed to it.

"Well, what about me?" she tried, unable to keep her longing gaze away from the tanned and powerful male body standing in front of her. "Think about what you're doing to me!"

"I don't have to think about that. You've already done your own thinking and set your own price. I'm willing to pay it. What could be simpler?"

He put one knee on the bed and reached for her. Panicked, Dara wriggled backward, getting shakily to her feet on the opposite side. She retreated swiftly, convinced he would pounce at her.

But he didn't move. Instead, Yale sat patiently on the edge of the bed and watched her with persuasive, gleaming eyes. His voice was unbelievably dark and silky on her nerves.

"Don't run from me, my darling Dara. Haven't I agreed to give you everything you've asked for? What more can a man do? I want you. Badly enough to pay your price. And you know you want me. Come here and let me show you. . . ."

She felt her senses reeling at the seductive tendrils curling around her and she knew she was going to be caught up in the spell of him as she had been last night. How could a woman deny the man she loved? It was like denying her own breath. It went against all her natural instincts. *And he was going to marry her!*

"Come here, little tabby cat," he coaxed with electrifying tenderness. "Come and warm me with your passion and your need. I want to feel the curve of your hips and the swell of your breasts. I want to know that moment when you lose control and give yourself completely. I want to feel you take me inside and make me a part of you. . . ."

"Oh, Yale," Dara whispered weakly, knowing her resistance was rapidly collapsing and helpless to stop it.

He held out his hand invitingly, and in spite of herself, Dara took a tentative step forward toward the bed. He was drawing her close with invisible bonds that had been forged last night and could never be unmade. She knew that in the deepest recesses of her mind. As long as Yale chose to chain her she was caught.

"I meant it, Yale," she tried valiantly as she stopped at the edge of the bed. His hand was still extended in silent demand. "I really meant it. If . . . if you go through with this I will expect nothing less than marriage!"

He moved then with unexpected swiftness, snagging

her wrist and pulling her down beside him. He rolled heavily onto her, crushing her into the quilt and gazing down into her startled eyes with masculine triumph.

"I never supposed you didn't," he assured her with a low groan of desire.

And then he was covering her mouth with his own, plundering the warmth he found there as if the previous night had only whetted his appetite. She was held fettered beneath his heavy strength while he mastered her senses once more.

"Yale, why do I let you do this to me?" Dara said huskily, coming alive under his touch.

"When you know the answer to that, tell me," he ordered gruffly.

Confident now of her willing compliance, Yale shifted, moving onto his back and pulling her into an abandoned sprawl across his chest. He slid the dress from her shoulders, past her waist, leaving her to kick free of the confining folds.

"You fill my hands so perfectly," he marveled, deftly unsnapping the front clasp of her bra and letting her soft femininity spill into his waiting hands.

Dara moaned deeply with mounting anticipation as her nipples rose to the touch of his thumb and forefinger. Unconsciously she arched her lower body against the pulsating maleness of him.

"Show me how an Oregon woman treats the man she's going to marry," Yale growled roughly, his hands moving down to her waist and over the curve of her hips, urging her closer.

Dara closed her eyes and gave herself over to the need they shared. Throwing any remaining caution to the winds, she allowed her love full rein.

Her lips sought his willingly, enticing a response that was granted immediately. She felt him groan as her breasts brushed teasingly against his chest, and his undisguised response encouraged her as nothing else could have done.

Her excitement scaling ever upward, Dara probed against the challenge of his tongue, defeating it utterly, and then she withdrew to explore the tips of his ears.

"You'll pay for that," he rasped in tantalizing menace as she carefully closed her teeth around one lobe. His fingertips sank sharply into her buttocks and scored a flickering pattern of excruciating, exhilarating stimulation which coursed down to her toes.

"Oh!" Dara's cry was one of feminine need and desire, and it seemed to act on him just as her hands and lips had acted.

But it also unleashed a totally unfamiliar aggression in her. A fantasy of power and seduction which Dara would never have dreamed she had. This man was hers. She had pushed him into a promise of marriage, a promise which she fully intended he should keep. He thought he was merely paying the price she had set, but there was more to it, much more. He was going to learn that he belonged to her, she decided exuberantly.

"My tabby cat is secretly a wildcat," Yale muttered in astonished wonder as Dara began a feverish exploration of his body. "My God, little one. You drive me crazy!"

She trailed kisses of damp passion down his throat, into the hollow of his shoulder and out to the sensitive inside of his elbow. His hands wrapped themselves in the heavy tangle of her hair as she kissed the warm skin of his stomach. His legs shifted heavily, restlessly, around her as she moved down to his thighs.

Once again she used her teeth, nipping with playful passion at the muscled tautness of him. She felt the rising desire that threatened to put an end to her bold loveplay and swiftly captured his wrists.

Dara was too caught up in the excitement and wonder of her newfound arrogance and aggression to realize she wasn't exactly mastering his strength with her own. The fact that he was submissive before her onslaught was enough. She would make him remember this night, she told herself as she moved upward again, straddling his hips and pinning his wrists beside his head.

"A wildcat," he grated hoarsely, not fighting the restraint of her hands as she leaned over to kiss him deeply, hungrily, persuasively. His body lifted, seeking hers, but she resisted, teasing him with a wantonness that amazed a small corner of her mind. This couldn't be her, that corner protested, quite shocked.

But it was, and Dara thrilled to the knowledge. She had known this man was crucial to her future happiness, but she had never dreamed he would open this door to her physical responses.

"Come and claim your man, woman!" Yale's soft command came tightly as she nibbled on his shoulder. She felt him arch upward again, urging her to complete the union.

But the wildness of her mood was not to be so easily coaxed back to the yielding Yale's body wanted. She would show this man he was at her mercy, make him acknowledge his desire for her. He would discover what it meant to be the one who submitted.

She lifted her head from his throat long enough to laugh a siren's laugh, gazing down into his gleaming hazel eyes.

"Do you want me, Yale?" she breathed.

"Want you, need you, desire you . . ." His head moved once on the pillow in silent disgust with the lack of sufficient words. Then he groaned with deep insistence. "Finish your seduction, tabby cat. Put me out of this misery. I can't stand your teasing much longer!"

"Misery?" She pouted, her fingertips toying with the masculine nipples. "I'm not sure I like that description. I wouldn't want to make you miserable, Yale. . . ."

"Call it what you want," he breathed huskily, "but finish it before I go out of my head!"

"I would like to see that." Dara laughed throatily, bending to touch her lips lightly to his throat. "I would like to see you driven a little crazy by me. . . ."

"You're enjoying your power?" he murmured, drawing in his breath sharply as she touched her tongue to the edge of his mouth and then his chin.

"Enormously."

"Have you ever played with fire before?" he demanded tightly.

"Not like this," she admitted.

"And now that you've chained a man in your spell, you're determined to extract all the pleasure from torturing him that you can, is that it?"

"I want to hear you beg," she agreed delightedly.

"I'm begging," he whispered.

"Not loudly enough." Still holding his wrists firmly to the bed, she scattered fleeting, alluring little kisses across his chest.

"You're a harsh mistress," he groaned.

"Not a mistress," she denied at once, angered slightly. "I'm going to be your wife!"

"In that case," he rapped suddenly, "you'd better start learning a little something about wifely obedience!"

He seemed to erupt beneath her, his hands coming free of her grip as if she had never attempted to bind him. Before she could do more than gasp her startled surprise, Dara found herself flat on her back, his broad shoulders looming over her.

Without warning she was thoroughly anchored to the bed, both her hands caught in one of his and drawn tautly over her head. His thigh moved over hers, pinning her writhing legs.

She felt the excitement flash through her in waves, as she reacted to the passionate capture with a thrilling awareness that was as strong as her previous sensation of power.

"Now, future wife," Yale gritted gently, his free hand beginning to move deliberately on her vulnerable midsection, "it's your turn to plead."

Dara smiled with dazzling witchcraft, her body already lifting against the touch of his hand. "Please, Yale. Please show me what being your wife will be like!"

"When you look at me like that, how can I refuse you anything?" he breathed, sliding his leg between hers with purposefulness and deliberate slowness.

He was going to keep her waiting, she realized dimly as she coiled and uncoiled beneath him. He wanted her to know the powerful need in every fiber of her being. She wanted to cry out her love for him, knew it was much too soon and cried out her desire instead.

"I want you, Yale. I want you so desperately!"

"I'm yours, sweetheart. I think I have been from the beginning!" He was poised above her in the darkness and then he was taking her with finesse and strength. She knew every inch of him along her skin, and her body vibrated in resonance with his.

He swept her along with him in the dizzying path of their mutual desire. Dara surrendered willingly to the demands he made of her, issuing her own demands in return. They were met with the same eagerness, and together they bounded toward the top of the cliff which overlooked the emerald valley.

Dara felt the shuddering release she had first known last night, still unprepared for the sensation even though she knew what to expect this time.

"Yale!"

Then he was leaping over the edge with her, a hoarse male shout caught in his throat as he slid a hand beneath her buttocks to hold her violently close. She felt him tremble, felt every muscle in his lean frame tauten. In that moment the taking and giving were so bound up together that it was impossible to speak of mastery and surrender. Each gave and each took. Each mastered and each surrendered. It was a timeless cadence which required only love to make it complete. And that Dara gave with all her heart, even if it was in silence.

It was a long time later, deep in the heavy aftermath of their passion, that Yale stirred and spoke softly, compellingly into the quiet darkness.

"You see, little tabby cat?" he said wistfully. "It doesn't really matter."

"What doesn't matter?" Dara murmured, luxuriating in the feel of him. She stretched like a cat beneath the soothing stroke of his hand.

"Where we come together like this," he explained. "A truck-stop motel or your bedroom or on a mountaintop overlooking the world. It's all the same. We're what counts, not the location."

She smiled against his damp skin and sighed blissfully. Secure in the knowledge that Yale couldn't have made love to her like this if he wasn't close to falling in love, she made her decision.

In the morning she would release him from his promise to marry her.

It was very simple, really, she told herself with catlike contentment. Yale would tell her he had no wish to be free of his promise and she would go to her wedding with the full knowledge that he wanted the marriage as much as she did.

How could it be otherwise after what they had shared?

Dara made her decision with the perfect certainty and confidence she had known when she finally realized she had discovered her niche in life as a stockbroker. Made it with all the absolute sureness with which she had first known she wanted to belong to Yale Ransom. Made it with a woman's sure instincts about herself and her man.

Yale would marry her because he wanted her, not because he was bound to a promise. And she would teach him to love her after the wedding.

Perhaps it was inevitable that such complacency should not go unpunished. But the inevitability did not lessen the heart-wrenching shock Dara experienced when Yale calmly accepted his freedom and grabbed it with both hands, making no effort to step back into the net.

7

~~~~~~~~~~~~~~~~~~~~

Okay."

That was his exact word the next morning when Dara, soft-eyed and full of love, told him she wouldn't hold him to the marriage promise. He was sliding out of bed, on his way to a shower in her eye-opening yellow and red bathroom.

"Okay!" she repeated to his disappearing back as the door closed. "Okay!" Dazed, she stared after him, unconsciously clutching the sheet over her full breasts. Only a short time ago he had awakened her with a kiss at the base of her spine, turned her over and made lazy, warm love to her.

And now he calmly shrugged and accepted his freedom as if he never had intended to marry her.

No! she told herself resolutely as she struggled free of the startled paralysis and got to her feet. Yale would have married her if she'd held him to his promise. She was sure of it. He was the sort of man who paid his debts!

But she'd blithely freed him of the obligation, and what

male in his right mind wouldn't be willing enough to accept that freedom? What a fool she had been! For the second morning in a row!

In that moment it was hard to know which of them was the more inviting target for her anger: herself or Yale.

Grabbing a turqoise robe from the closet, Dara flung it on and stalked into the bathroom. It was already turning into a steam bath from the hot water Yale was using in such liberal quantities.

"What the hell do you mean, 'okay'?" she demanded over the noise of the shower. She could see his shadowy movements behind the yellow curtain.

"Okay means okay," he called back laconically. "You set the price last night. If you don't want to collect full payment, that's your prerogative."

"The price! Is that all you ever think about? Yesterday you were willing to pay the price by handing over your account! This morning you were willing to . . . to marry me! Don't you mind the cost?" she bit out.

There was an instant's pause, and then Yale pulled back the shower curtain far enough to smile at her. There was a knee-weakening tenderness in the smile. There was also the devilish flash of gold.

"The fact that I'm willing to pay it should tell you how much I want you," he pointed out gently. "But if you're too generous to collect . . ." He let the sentence trail off significantly.

She glared at him, vividly aware of the way the water streamed across his head and shoulders, plastering the honey hair to his head and making the smooth, strong contours of his chest and arms glisten. She loved him, she acknowledged again, glumly, and he was playing games with her. He had been from the beginning. She had no one to blame but herself.

And at last, two mornings too late, everything crystallized. She had fallen in love at first sight with a man who returned the physical attraction, but nothing deeper. It wasn't altogether his fault, either. She had allowed the situation to race out of control. She had succumbed to him so easily there had been no time for Yale to get to know her as a human being. On his demand during the past forty-eight hours she had handed over everything of herself with only token resistance. He was honest enough to be willing to pay her price, but he hadn't fallen in love.

With the cool, clear assessment of hindsight, Dara realized finally what she had done. At the age of thirty she should know enough about men to realize they didn't fall head over heels in love at first sight. A man's emotions were far more primitive. Men were quite capable of wanting a woman and wanting her badly after a short acquaintance, but falling in love was a much more complicated and lengthy business.

If there was to be any hope for her relationship with Yale Ransom, Dara told herself with chilling caution, she would have to go back to the beginning and start the relationship from scratch.

She drew a deep breath and smiled back at the man in her shower, a smile unlike any he'd had from her so far. A smile few people ever saw.

"It's not that I'm too generous," she began with icy sarcasm. He arched an eyebrow, waiting for the other shoe to drop. "But I am much too smart to let the emotions of a wild weekend lead me into making a major mistake. We've only known each other for two days, Yale. Marriage would be a horrendous mistake. I only said that last night to try to stop you from seducing me." She shrugged with deliberate self-mockery. "But you're good. Very good."

Something moved in the depths of the hazel eyes, but the wicked smile still played about his hard mouth. "Thank you for the compliment. I shall do my best to continue to live up to the expectations I've created."

She'd struck some sort of nerve, but Dara couldn't begin to figure out what was going on in his mind now.

He had a certain watchfulness about him. As if he were paying out rope and waiting to see how much she would take before she obligingly hanged herself.

"I'm sure you will," she acknowledged politely. "With some other woman."

"I'm content with the one I've got," he drawled, ignoring the hot water which was being wasted by the gallon. He was deliberately challenging her, and Dara felt more than ready for the battle.

"How kind of you," she murmured. "My turn to accept the compliment, I suppose. But I'm afraid I have other plans for other weekends. This one has been . . . interesting, to say the least, but not something I intend to make a practice of repeating."

"No?" The single word was edged with humor and a masculine certainty that annoyed Dara.

"No," she replied very calmly. Then she glanced down the front of her fluffy robe, taking in her figure with an amused expression. "I'm aware of the fact that men sometimes get the notion I'm a little . . . soft . . ."

"And cuddly?" he added helpfully, following her glance with an assessing one of his own.

"And cuddly," she agreed with a rueful sigh. "I haven't given you much reason to think otherwise, either. But I'm afraid the body nature gave me doesn't totally reflect the whole woman."

"What's hidden?" he asked lightly. "What haven't I already seen?"

"Believe it or not, I can be extraordinarily stubborn." She chuckled.

"Are you trying to tell me in your own devious fashion that you're not going to sleep with me again?" he demanded, looking fascinated.

"For a country boy, you're quite sharp at times." She smiled.

He ignored that. "What makes you think I can't make last night and the night before happen again and again?"

"Once I've made a decision and know what I'm doing, I'm quite unswerving." That was nothing less than the truth.

"You said something like this yesterday morning, as I recall."

"No," she responded coolly. "Yesterday morning I was madder than hell. It was inevitable I should get over that. I never stay angry long." She smiled reminiscently. "And you were very pleasant last night."

"You're not trying to retaliate for some imagined slight this morning?"

"Nope. I'm merely trying to tell you that the weekend is coming to an end."

"And if I said I wanted to go on seeing you?" he prodded, the smallest hint of impatience in his words.

"I'd tell you that you're welcome to call. Just don't expect to spend the night again."

"Why not?"

"Because, in spite of the impression I'm afraid you've gotten this weekend, I don't leap into casual affairs."

"The past forty-eight hours represent a temporary aberration, is that it?" he retorted broodingly.

"It happens to all of us on occasion." She sighed wryly. "But that doesn't mean one has to make a practice of it. If you want to continue seeing me, Yale, I'm willing. I enjoy your company. But I give you fair warning that I'm putting this weekend behind me, where it belongs, and returning to reality."

He watched her for a heartbeat and then he said very softly, "Come here, Dara."

She tilted her head, wary of his intentions. "Why?"

"I want to show you something."

"I can see all I need to see from here," she muttered, refusing to let her gaze slip farther than his chest. She wished he would close the curtain.

"Scared?"

"Of course not!"

"Then come a little closer, honey," he urged persuasively.

"Yale, I'd like you to hurry and get out of that shower so you can be on your way before my neighbors are all awake," she instructed him resolutely, turning on her heel and opening the bathroom door.

He closed in on her as her hand came down on the doorknob. Dripping wet, he pulled her around and whipped the fluffy robe off her shoulders.

"Yale! You're getting water all over the floor! What do you think you're doing?" Her protest was a startled squeak of alarm that didn't seem to faze him in the least.

"There are a few more things we need to discuss," he told her, forcing her now nude body into the shower ahead of him. "And something tells me we'll communicate better this way!"

"Stop it!" she snapped even as the hot water drenched her. "I'm in no mood for any of your games!"

"Speaking of games," he began easily, wrapping one arm around her breasts and holding her still while he industriously began to scrub her back, "just what sort do you think you're playing this morning?"

She felt his strong hands working steadily down her tapering back, moving slickly on her wet skin, and she wanted to give herself up to the sensuous moment. But that was impossible. Too much was riding on her will-power, and once the Bancroft will of iron had been invoked, nothing could bend it.

"What games?" she charged tightly. "I've told you not to assume from this weekend that I'm willing to engage in a full-scale affair with you. That's all!"

"You've also told me you're no longer interested in collecting the fee for last night's charming surrender. Funny, I could have sworn at the time you had every intention of doing so!"

He soaped the contour of her waist and then, tantalizingly, began to make slippery forays over her hips. Helpless in his one-armed grip, Dara steeled herself against the onslaught.

"It was not a surrender, damn it," she grated, knowing her temper was beginning to fray under the pressure. "I don't know how things work back in the mountains, but out here on the Coast, women occasionally go to bed with men because they feel like it! It doesn't constitute a surrender in any sense of the word!"

"Then why the insistence on marriage?" he retorted, his fingers gliding more slowly now as he shaped the resilient flesh of her buttocks. "If you were only going to bed with me because I took your fancy for the moment, why demand marriage?"

"I told you, I was trying to stop you from seducing me!"

"You didn't have the willpower to simply say no?" he taunted.

"Not then," she admitted grimly. "But I do now. The weekend, Yale, is over!"

"I've got news for you, sweetheart," he growled, turning her in his arms and staring down into her upturned face without smiling. "It's just beginning. I want you now. You've pushed your way into my life. Seduced me would be a better term, I suppose. You know more about me than anyone else has known for years. You've given me just enough of your lovely, soft body to make me want a lot more, and you've let me see what I can do to you. One weekend isn't going to satisfy me. I was willing to pay for what I want with marriage, but if you don't want that, there isn't any way I can force you into it. I'll take what's left, which is an affair."

"Not on your life!" she flared, eyes burning an emerald color as she defied him.

His hands were around her waist, moving upward until his thumbs found the rosy tips of her breasts. "You don't

115

mean that," he whispered deeply, circling the sensitive nipples deliberately. "You've already said I could continue seeing you. . . ."

"You can," she flung back icily. "But if you want to date me, Yale, you must understand that this relationship is going back to square one. You would have to forget about the weekend and pretend we had just met."

"What man could forget a weekend like this?" he asked huskily, bending down beneath the hot spray to drop a knowing little kiss on her forehead.

"I know it's all my fault," Dara groaned, closing her eyes.

"Very generous of you to take the blame," he commended, his lips moving to her temples.

"I let things get out of control," she went on sadly. "I handled it completely wrong, I admit that."

"And now you're going to try and retreat to a position where you can handle it properly, is that it?" He chuckled, his hands cupping her breasts with increasing urgency.

"Yes!" she vowed.

"Such determination," he drawled with lazy interest. She knew he was becoming aroused again. His stamina was a little frightening!

"When I finally get around to making a decision, Yale, nothing can change my mind."

"And you've decided you let me go too far, too fast?"

"Exactly."

"It's done, honey," he said silkily, propelling her closer until she could feel the sexual tautness in him. "You can't go back. . . ."

"I'm thirty years old, Yale Ransom," she announced with cool fortitude. "I can do anything I damn please!"

Whirling so quickly she caught him by surprise, Dara stepped away from his slippery hold and out onto the rug. She grabbed the nearest towel and hurriedly pulled it around her dripping body. He tugged back the curtain once more and stood regarding her for all the world like an annoyed shark which has just lost its prey. Did sharks have hazel eyes that gleamed like the gold in their teeth?

"I don't understand you this morning," he complained, sounding aggrieved.

"Precisely my point," she flung back, starting for the door again. "The problem with wild weekends is that the activities tend to be too limited in scope. We've made a lot of love during the past two days, Yale, but you know almost nothing about me. The only reason I've learned something about you is because I kept pressing for information. We're still a long way from genuine communication. I should have had the sense to realize that too much sex too early in a relationship severely hampers the task of getting to know each other! Frankly, I'm not interested in a relationship based solely on the physical side of things!"

With royal disdain, Dara slammed out of the bathroom. Her mind was made up. The future path lay as sharply marked before her as if it were lit with neon lights.

She was dressed in jeans and a snappy plaid shirt, cracking eggs into a skillet, when Yale emerged from the bathroom and came to lean in the kitchen doorway. She ignored his appraising glance even though it seemed to burn through the fabric of her shirt.

"So you're at least going to feed me before kicking me out, hmm?"

"Don't knock it. I'm a good cook." Dara surveyed the toast with a watchful eye. "The Sunday paper's over there on the table if you want to occupy yourself while I'm fixing breakfast."

"Very homey," he muttered dryly as he detached himself from the doorframe and wandered over to the round glass table by the kitchen window. He stood beside the fern on the tall plant stand and scanned the headlines, hazel eyes narrowed behind the lenses of his glasses.

Eyeing him covertly, Dara knew his mind wasn't on the morning news. Encouraged, she poured a cup of coffee and carried it over to him. He looked up as he accepted the mug, the grooves around the edges of his mouth tight.

"Dara, about last night . . ."

"How do you like your eggs? Over easy or sunny-side up?"

"I don't much care at the moment," he rapped. "I'm trying to talk to you about us, damn it!"

"So talk. I'm listening."

She turned away, opened a kitchen drawer and began dragging out flatware. Yale flung himself into a chair and watched morosely as she set the table with smooth, efficient movements. She could sense him searching for the words he wanted.

"Honey, we can't calmly go back to the beginning and start over," he finally began in an eminently reasonable tone of voice that made her want to smile: the rational male was attempting to deal with the irrational female.

"Then we can call it quits right here," she said easily. "Or we can maintain a business relationship, I suppose— that is, if you still want to give Edison, Stanford and Zane your account. There, that's at least two other alternatives I can think of at the moment," she concluded brightly, dishing up the bacon and eggs and toast.

"I have no intention of following either suggestion!" he growled as she set the food in front of him.

"Then you can go back to the beginning and we can start from scratch. Take your pick." She sat down opposite him and shot Yale a dazzling smile as she picked up her fork.

He watched her through narrowed lids, the fingers of his right hand drumming with ill-concealed impatience on the cheerful striped tablecloth.

"What if I agree to do that and then prove you can't resist me?" he offered coolly.

His self-confidence hardened her resolve as nothing else could have done. "You mean agree to start over and then deliberately seduce me? It wouldn't work. Not now. I've made up my mind, Yale. You haven't known me long enough to realize exactly what that means. We'll go as far as I want, and then I'll send you home. Just as I would any other date."

"Are you issuing a challenge?" he asked, finally picking up his fork, unable to ignore his food any longer.

"No, I'm telling you how it's going to be between us, Yale," she explained patiently. "I want a normal, properly developed relationship, or I want nothing at all. As interesting as this weekend has been, it was a mistake. It won't happen again."

"You're very sure of yourself this morning. Yesterday morning you were in a flaming rage," he noted calmly.

"Yes," she agreed, her mouth quirking wryly. "I was. But when I'm in a rage, which is rather rare, I'm not at my most dangerous. It's when I'm cool, organized and know where I'm going next that I'm a force to contend with."

"I'll remember that," he vowed, lifting his coffee cup.

"You certainly will," she promised sweetly. "More coffee?"

He held out his cup without a word. She could practically see him turning over her responses in his mind.

"You want the Southern gentleman back, is that it?" he asked finally. "You like the man you met at the party but not the one you found yourself with in a motel room out on the Interstate?"

"Stop trying to pretend you're two different men, Yale. Both aspects of you are part of the whole. There's no point trying to deny one or the other. Actually"—she smiled warmly—"they go together rather nicely."

He looked a little taken aback, as if he hadn't expected

such an admission. But he was quick to seize on the apparent weakness. "If you're attracted to both sides of me," he pounced, "why are you so determined to keep me at bay?"

"Being attracted to a man is not a good enough reason for having an affair with him!"

"Why not?"

"Spoken with the essence of male logic." She groaned, shaking her head so that the russet ends, still damp from her unplanned slower, danced around her throat. "The female's reasoned response to which is *because it's not!*"

"Careful, Dara," he clipped, stabbing his egg vengefully. "I'm tempted to meet your response to my logic by turning you over my knee!"

"Now, that wouldn't be very reasonable, would it?" she murmured.

"I think you've been reading too much of that eighteenth-century philosophy I saw on your bookshelf. Just remember that back during the seventeen hundreds, during the so-called Age of Reason, it was still legal to beat one's wife! A very practical era."

"Ah! But I'm not your wife!" she murmured triumphantly, lowering her lashes to hide the mischief in her eyes.

"No," he agreed on a distant note. "You backed out of your deal the minute you woke up this morning. But I'm not at all willing to do the same. I want you, little tabby cat, and I can make you want me."

"The only way you can continue to see me is on my terms," she stated aloofly. "This weekend is simply not going to be allowed to set the tone of our relationship, and that's final."

"You *are* issuing a challenge," he accused, waving his fork at her briefly.

"The fact that you can say that only goes to show how little you know me."

"It won't work," he told her darkly.

"Our relationship?"

"Trying to put it on another footing," he elaborated. "It won't work."

"Then that will be the end of things."

"I accept," he gritted.

"Accept what?"

"The challenge. To put it in elemental terms, I will prove I can seduce you and make you eat every last one of your fine words. Before I'm finished you will be begging me to marry you!"

Dara forced down the excitement wafting through her senses. She was a long way from the finish line yet. With seeming casualness she raised her coffee cup in mocking salute.

"Is that the Southern gentleman or the moonshine runner talking?"

"That's *me*, Yale Ransom, talking, and I mean every word! Whatever else happened this weekend, the one abiding fact is that I made you mine. I'm going to make you admit it if it's the last thing I do on this earth!"

"Fine," she said easily. "Now, if you don't mind, would you hurry up and finish that coffee? I'd like to get you out of this apartment as quickly as possible. With any luck maybe the neighbors won't notice the Alfa Romeo. . . ."

"Are you that worried about being compromised?" he jeered.

"As you said last night, I'd probably survive it, but there's no sense deliberately inviting any more trouble, is there?"

"Speaking of which," he interrupted loftily, "what about the business with Hank Bonner's drug runner?" His smile was one of impending victory. "I still feel morally obligated to look after you as long as he's on the loose."

"Try looking at page A12 in this morning's paper," she invited kindly.

Shooting her a glaring frown, Yale flipped open the paper.

"It's in fine print close to the bottom of the page under the advertisement for tennis rackets."

His mouth moved into a harder line as he read the brief report. "So they got him last night, after all."

"He never stood a chance, what with all those truckers looking for him."

"And we're in the clear," he continued absently, finishing the few lines announcing the arrest of a man suspected of using interstate truckers to transport drugs.

"No mention of us at all." Dara grinned cheerfully. "Your reputation as a nice, staid, gentlemanly accountant is safe."

"And your habit of getting involved in barroom brawls and then going off into the night with a trucker or two is also safely hidden. It looks like we'll both be able to show our faces in downtown Eugene tomorrow."

"Something tells me you weren't as worried as you pretended to be about your reputation," she murmured, rising to clear away his plate in a pointed manner. She didn't offer him another cup of coffee.

"Were you?" he asked suddenly, looking up speculatively. "Would you have gone ahead and married me if we'd been made to look like a pair of reckless swingers?"

"It's an interesting problem, isn't it? We'll never know the answer, I'm afraid." She flicked a quick smile at him, mentally shouting, Yes! Yes! I probably would have been tempted by that excuse. My reputation wouldn't have mattered as much as having a legitimate excuse for marrying you. But I haven't even got that now. And I want you to marry me for far more important reasons, Yale Ransom. I want you to fall in love with me the way I've fallen in love with you!

"The answer might have been amusing," he drawled, sliding reluctantly to his feet, "but perhaps not as amusing as watching you trying to fend me off when you know you'll be aching to have me. . . ."

Before he'd finished the last word, Yale had reached out and slid his arms around her waist as she stood at the sink. She went very still, bracing herself against the counter.

"Yale, it's time for you to go," she said steadily as he hugged her back against his strength.

"Don't worry, honey, I'm on my way," he whispered huskily into her hair. "I told you, I've accepted the challenge. You can't go back to square one. We know too much about each other. We're lovers, Dara. We're going to stay lovers. You want me and I want you. Life is really very simple in some ways."

"A bit of Blue Ridge Mountain wisdom?" she murmured.

"A bit of Yale Ransom wisdom. And a young woman who didn't have enough sense to resist opening Pandora's box ought to pay attention. Because she's going to take all the consequences of her actions!"

His hands dropped away from her waist, leaving her feeling bereft. Dara spun around to watch as Yale strode out of the kitchen. She followed and stood in the doorway as he found his jacket and walked to the front door.

"Goodbye, lover," he called, letting himself out into the early-morning sunshine. "I'll be seeing you soon. You can count on it!"

She raced to the window and watched as he moved down the walk to the waiting car. As he settled into the front seat he turned and waved again. Even from here she could see the menace in his smile.

As the Alfa Romeo pulled away from the curb, Yale's hand was once again extended from the window. But this time he wasn't waving at her. He was acknowledging the gray-haired woman across the street who was peering eagerly through her kitchen blinds.

Dara muttered a decidedly violent oath and let her own curtains fall back into place. What was it they said about the devil living in those Southern mountains? She seemed to recall some old tales. Tales that sent chills of warning down her nerves.

Well, the devil was going to meet his match in her, she vowed silently.

A long time later as she whizzed along the bike path beside the Willamette River, letting the spring sunshine put the world back into proportion for her sadly chaotic senses, Dara tried to imagine Yale's mood. Automatically she shifted the gears of her ten-speed.

Was he frustrated the way a tiger is frustrated when its prey is rudely snatched from its jaws just after the feast has begun? Was he angry over her exposure of his past? He certainly hadn't been too pleased when she'd pushed him into revealing it.

Whatever his reasoning at the moment, she had the satisfaction of knowing he was going to play the dangerous game for which she was setting the rules.

Only now, in the clear light of day as she sped through one of Eugene's many parks, could she admit to herself how reckless she had really been.

Not because she had spent a "lost" weekend with a man she had barely met, but because she had risked letting him back out of the net after she'd secured him with a promise of marriage. Would she ever make him understand, or would he be more wary this time?

She was under no illusions about his determination to go on seeing her. She had deliberately challenged him, and his instincts had prompted him to accept. He'd even realized what she was doing and he'd still accepted, she reminded herself with a smile.

What he didn't realize was that she wasn't going to let

RECKLESS PASSION

him win. It was too important for both their sakes that she control the next crucial moves.

Dara knew she would be satisfied with nothing less than Yale Ransom's love. She was too proud, too determined, to settle for anything short of it. Once before she had done that, and she wasn't going to let it happen again.

She might have gotten the love affair off to a shaky start by allowing herself to be swept up into a reckless and dangerous forty-eight hours, but she would salvage the disaster or lose everything trying. Once Dara Bancroft knew what she wanted in life, she went after it.

8

The hunt began the next day, and almost immediately Dara knew she had underestimated Yale's natural stalking skill. But who could have guessed that she would find herself the quarry of a split personality?

The first appeared shortly before her lunch hour on Monday. The conservative, gently spoken, fine-mannered Southern gentleman walked through the front door of Edison, Stanford & Zane, nodded to the secretary and strolled over to Dara's desk.

"Good morning, Dara." He smiled politely, only the hint of gold betraying the true nature of the expression. "I've got all the information here that you'll need to transfer the account from L.A."

Dara looked up a little warily, not quite trusting this genteel version of his accent. She was aware that more than one head in the office had turned in amused curiosity.

"Fine, Yale, won't you have a seat?" she murmured

126

politely, indicating one of the client chairs in front of her desk. She reached for the sheaf of papers he extended. "I'll see to these today."

He settled his neatly suited leanness into the chair and the hazel eyes were full of laughter which the lenses of his glasses failed to hide.

"I've got some time, so I thought I'd stop by and discuss my financial goals in the market. Always a good idea for client and broker to feel each other out, so to speak, don't you think?" he drawled politely.

"Of course," she agreed briskly, reaching for a pad and pen. She could play this every bit as cool as he could. It was, after all, her idea, damn it!

"I see your portfolio emphasizes growth stocks," she observed in her best professional tones, glancing at his statement from the other firm. "I gather you're not concerned with income producers?"

"I have no need of dividends. I'm looking for the long-term-growth stocks. Find me a few dozen bargains in the over-the-counter market and I'll be satisfied," he said easily.

"Bargains?" She half smiled. "What's your definition of a bargain?"

"Why, something that doubles or triples in the first year, naturally," Yale explained kindly.

"And you expect a few dozen such winners from me?" she inquired coolly.

"Your manager assures me you're good. Very good." He met her eyes, daring her to deny it.

"I am, but I'm not perfect." She smiled aloofly. "I happen to be following a couple of interesting electronics stocks at the moment, however. They're down from their highs for the year and selling at rather good P/E ratios. There's also a small cable television firm which hasn't been 'discovered' yet but which I think will really go places. Would you like to see some information?"

"I would be most interested in discussing all of them further. Over lunch? It is just after one o'clock, I believe. The markets should be closed back East. . . ."

Dara slanted her new client a cautious glance. Yale was on his best behavior at the moment, but the humor in his eyes held more than simple amusement. The expression was compounded by something else, something she couldn't quite put her finger on but which the common-sense portion of her brain warned against.

"I'll have to be back in an hour," she began carefully. "I have a lot of work to do this afternoon. . . ."

"I'll have you back by two. You have my word on it. I should be back in my own office shortly after that, myself." He got to his feet expectantly.

Dara hesitated and then took the plunge. This was what she wanted, wasn't it? Time for them to get to know each other on other levels besides the physical?

"I'll get my coat," she said calmly.

Whatever it was that was sending tiny warnings along her spine failed to materialize over lunch in a downtown restaurant. Yale was the complete and perfect escort, attentive, polite and charming. Slowly, as she worked her way through a large salad, Dara began to relax. If this was going to be his approach, she could handle it. It was exactly the sort of relationship she wanted at the moment.

"You never did tell me what you did for a living before you became an account executive with Edison, Stanford and Zane," Yale said invitingly at one point.

"A great many things, I'm afraid. My résumé reads like the want-ads column. You name it and I probably tried it." Dara smiled at him, remembering her frequent job-hops. "I worked in an insurance office, a department store, a travel agency, a temporary secretarial help firm, city government, a restaurant, a hotel, an airline—"

"Okay," he interrupted, chuckling, "I get the picture. Is selling stocks merely another passing job interest?"

"Oh, no," she said in surprise. "Selling securities is what I wanted to do all along. I just didn't know it until I stumbled onto it," she explained.

"How do you know you won't lose interest and go on to something else?"

She lifted a shoulder, helpless to explain her instinctive knowledge of the rightness of some things in her life. "I know," she said, smiling. "I just know." The same way that I know I love you, she thought.

"You sound very certain," Yale said quietly, giving her an oblique look.

"I am. I've always been like that, going from one thing to another until something clicks. But when it does click, I know it instantly. I stick with it. For example, Eugene clicked after I moved here from Portland."

"Did your first marriage seem to click?" he asked softly, a little relentlessly.

Dara's eyes hardened for a second and then she relaxed. "No. But I was a lot younger then and I hadn't learned to pay attention to all the important clicks or lack thereof."

"Were you passionately in love?"

"I was . . . infatuated, I suppose, is the word. He was very charming, very amusing and kind. I *liked* him. How can I explain it? I thought we had a lot in common and I thought we could make a go of it."

"But there was no 'click'?" Yale pressed deliberately.

"No. There was no click," she admitted.

"Has there ever been someone with whom everything feels right? Will you know it if it does happen?" he prodded, hazel eyes flickering with an enigmatic expression.

"Yes, to both questions," she said as lightly as possible. "But I'd rather not discuss it."

The amusement faded completely from his eyes as Yale studied her speculatively. "Where is he now? What happened to the relationship?"

"I told you, I'd rather not discuss it," Dara said with the serene sureness she was capable of projecting when she had made up her mind.

"Was he married? Does he live here in Eugene?"

"Yale, I'm not going to discuss it with you. Hadn't you better finish your steak? It's getting late."

"Dara . . ." he began determinedly, leaning forward with a surprisingly grim resolve. "Tell me about him.

"No. I'm ready to go, Yale. Are you going to take me back to the office, or shall I walk?"

"Did you run off into the night with him within a few hours of meeting him? The way you ran off with me?"

"Goodbye, Yale. I'll call you when I get the account transferred. In the meantime, I'll send you the information on those electronics firms I mentioned. . . ." Dara was getting to her feet, smoothing the white skirt of her suit with a casual hand and reaching for her fawn-colored shoulder bag.

He stood up at once, and she could almost see the restraint he flung around himself like a cloak.

"I'll take you back," he muttered with determined politeness.

"Careful, Yale," she taunted gently. "The Southern gentleman is slipping a little."

"I'll behave," he promised, guiding her out of the restaurant with a hand on her waist. "Although I'll have to admit it was never this hard before I met you."

"Keep up the good work. I'm rather fond of you when you're good. You make a very charming escort."

His mouth twisted wryly as he held the car door for her. "In that case, will you have dinner with me tomorrow night?"

Dara smiled. "I'd be delighted." Privately, she wondered why the invitation hadn't been for this evening. But it was just as well. She had a variety of things to do, anyway.

He drove her back to the office in an almost meditative

silence. The Alfa Romeo slid neatly into the curb in front of Edison, Stanford & Zane, and Dara's hand automatically went to the door handle.

"Thank you for lunch, Yale," she began with mocking formality and then stopped as his hand left the wheel to settle purposefully on her arm. She glanced down at his gripping fingers and then back up into his eyes with a questioning smile on her mouth.

"A little something to help you remember me by until tomorrow night," he said huskily and pulled her close for an unexpected kiss.

Before Dara could make up her mind how to respond, it was over. She fumbled briefly with the handle and jumped out of the car. "Goodbye, Yale!" She didn't turn her head as the car reentered traffic.

All things considered, it hadn't been a bad beginning, Dara decided several hours later as she stopped by the supermarket on the way home. Yale had been firmly in his Southern-gentleman role that afternoon. Perhaps he had determined to charm her back into bed. She smiled ruefully to herself at the thought. Perhaps she would allow him to do exactly that. After she'd decided he felt something more for her than simple desire.

She pushed the cart quickly down the aisle, scooping up milk and butter and other essentials from the dairy case. With a small frown she deliberated over dinner and decided on pasta. She would pick up some cheese and then . . .

Her train of thought halted abruptly as something familiar flickered at the corner of her vision. Curiously she turned her head to glance back down the aisle.

Yale stood at the far end dressed in black, close-fitting slacks and a black, long-sleeved shirt. He was watching her, his hands thrust into his back pockets, feet slightly apart and braced. The honey-amber hair was ruffled from the wind and he wasn't wearing his glasses.

"Yale!" Dara whispered in astonishment, smiling automatically and starting forward with the cart. What a coincidence, she mused.

He gave no sign of recognition, merely turned and disappeared around the corner of the aisle. When Dara reached the spot where he had been standing there was no sign of him.

Confused, Dara peered around and glanced out through the windows into the parking lot. Where had he gone? And why hadn't he waited to greet her? It *had* been Yale, hadn't it?

Of course it had, she reassured herself with a little shake of her head. Perhaps he hadn't seen her. With a shrug, Dara continued to the checkout stand.

Some time later she finished off her pasta with satisfaction. Dara had never allowed herself to fall into the trap of giving her dinner only minimal attention just because she happened to be eating alone. Her single place setting by the window was properly set with a glass of good wine and pretty china. Food was one of life's great pleasures and she refused to treat it as mundane.

She rose slowly to do the few dishes, her mind still churning with thoughts of Yale as it had been all afternoon. Idly she considered what she would wear the next evening and wondered if he would make a pass at her front door. The notion amused her in some ways, made her nervous in others.

But she could handle him, she told herself resolutely. Yale Ransom was going to learn that she wanted a real relationship or nothing at all. There would be no more wild, lost weekends!

She was still telling herself that when she finally slipped beneath the quilt of her bed and snuggled down to sleep. She had made up her mind, and once that had been done, she reminded herself firmly, nothing could change it.

The sound of a guitar woke her an hour later. For a moment Dara simply lay quietly, eyes still shut, and tried to remember if she'd left the stereo on earlier in the evening. She must have. The music was so close it couldn't be coming from a neighbor's apartment.

But why hadn't the stereo shut itself off automatically? her sleep-clogged brain demanded. Reluctantly her dark lashes fluttered open and she gazed at the pattern of moonlight on the far wall of her room. The guitar sounded so close, not at all as if it were seeping in from the living room. . . .

The panic hit her like a crashing wave, driving her up into a sitting position against the pillows. In the darkness she saw the devil, dressed in black, sitting on the end of her bed and strumming the guitar.

"Yale!" She choked on a small scream. "My God! What are you doing here? You scared the life out of me!"

She clutched the sheet to her throat, her pulse pounding, and glared at him accusingly.

"I'm really much better with a fiddle," Yale confided softly, glancing up from the movements of his fingers on the strings.

"Yes, I can imagine!" she retorted on an infuriated shriek. "I believe your Southern mountain devil does play a fiddle!"

"Only when he's bargaining for souls." Yale grinned, the gold flashing wickedly.

In that moment it wouldn't have taken much at all to convince Dara that she was facing Lucifer himself.

"How did you get in? What in the world do you think you're doing?"

"Frightened?" He smiled, still picking out a mountain ballad as he lounged at ease on her quilt.

"You terrified me, and you know it! Now answer me, Yale!" she charged.

He was dressed as he had been that afternoon when she'd glimpsed him in the store. There was no sign of the horn-rimmed glasses. He was all dark, lazy menace.

"I'm here to serenade you to sleep," he murmured.

133

"As for getting in, that was simple. I came through a window."

"Of all the nerve! Yale, what are you up to? This is . . . this is insane! And why didn't you speak to me in the store this afternoon?" she added belligerently as an afterthought.

He struck a few more chords on the guitar and then changed to another haunting melody, his amber head bent over the instrument.

"This afternoon? There was no need. I only wanted you to know I was there."

"But why?" Perplexed and a little angry, Dara sat very still, trying to figure out what he was doing.

"The quarry starts getting nervous when it realizes the hunter is right behind it. If there was one thing I learned to do back in those mountains, it was hunt."

"Hunt! Are you out of your mind? I'm not going to let you hunt me down like some helpless animal!" she blazed, thoroughly incensed.

"I'll get to you somehow," he told her gently, looking at her through his lashes. "Either me or my alter ego."

"Will you stop talking as if you're two separate men?" she flashed, a shiver going through her whole body at the quiet certainty in him.

"Well," he told her casually, the soft rhythms of the guitar reaching insidiously into every corner of the room, "you're the only one who can bring them together."

"This is ridiculous," she stormed, pushing a curve of russet hair back behind one ear and glaring at her uninvited guest. "If you think I'm going to tolerate this sort of behavior—"

"The first thing you're going to have to do is keep your tactics straight," he cautioned helpfully. "The ranting and raving might work on the Southern gentleman. After all, he would hate to distress a lady. But they aren't effective against the man sitting on the foot of your bed tonight."

"Really?" she shot back fiercely. "Then what do you suggest?"

"Sweet, soft submission, I think," Yale said reflectively as if seriously considering the issue.

"When hell freezes over!"

"Let's find out if your approach will work," he drawled, setting aside the guitar and sliding off the quilt.

The prickling sensation along her nerve endings exploded into full-scale alarm as Yale came toward her.

"Yale, no! I won't let you . . . !"

He sat down heavily beside her and reached out to pull her into his arms. She struggled, still trying to maintain her hold on the sheet, but he ignored her efforts, cradling her across his thighs.

"Go on fighting me, darling Dara, and we'll see where it gets you," he whispered, sweeping the sheet out of her grasp with a short, aggressive movement.

His hand came to rest just below the full curve of her breast and then began slipping down the satiny material of her nightgown.

"Stop that," she breathed tightly, trying to push against his chest with all her strength. "This isn't going to work, Yale Ransom. I'm not going to tamely let you seduce me!"

"Tame is a word I would never apply to you, sweetheart," he assured her as his fingers trailed lightly over her thigh. He anchored her arms against her sides and bent to kiss her angrily parted lips.

"No!"

But the word was lost in a muffled shout as his tongue forged into the warmth of her mouth. Effortlessly he held her still for the heavy, drugging kiss and the marauding quest of his hand.

Dara gathered her resistance, aware she couldn't fight him physically. He was simply too strong. But she would see to it that he gained no satisfaction from his bold lovemaking tonight. If there was one thing Dara Bancroft could do, it was to follow through on a project once she'd finally decided what had to be done.

Grimly she lay acquiescent beneath his touch, calling on her total store of willpower to turn off the electric circuits his hands and mouth switched on. Never again was Yale Ransom going to think of her as an easy conquest!

"Relax, honey," he breathed encouragingly as he began a series of slow, lingering kisses down the length of her throat. "Remember how good it was when you gave yourself to me? You know you want that again. . . ."

"It won't work, Yale," she hissed, turning her face into the black material of his shirt as his exploring hand slipped under the edge of her nightgown and found the silky skin of her inner thigh.

He said nothing but continued the patterns he was weaving on her skin, his fingers probing ever closer to the secret heart of her desire with knowing ease.

"I've learned a lot about you during the past couple of days," he told her insinuatingly. "I know how your body responds to my touch, how warm and soft and welcoming it becomes. . . ."

"I've warned you before that the body I was given doesn't reflect the mind behind it!" she challenged, stiffening herself against his touch.

He kissed the nape of her neck and then sank his teeth gently into the skin of her shoulder. "I think it does," he countered when he felt her tremor of response. "Tell me the truth, Dara. Can't you hear the click of everything falling into place when you lie in my arms?"

"No, Yale, there are too many missing factors still. . . ."

But she was lying and she knew it. The click had been resounding and final the moment she'd looked up into his eyes that night at the party.

"What's missing, sweetheart?" he asked persuasively

between kisses as he worked his way down the slope of her breast to the lacy edge of the nightgown. "Tell me and I'll provide it."

"You've already proved you'll say anything you have to say to get what you want," she swore bitterly. "You even agreed to marriage the last time!"

"But you didn't hold me to the agreement," he pointed out. "Why was that, I wonder? What made you change your mind about our bargain?"

"It was never meant as a bargain! I only wanted to find some way of stopping you!"

"I would have abided by it," he drawled, withdrawing his hand from her inner thigh momentarily to pull back the bodice of her nightgown.

"I'm flattered," she ground out furiously, aware of her breast being slowly, deliciously exposed.

"You should be. I don't marry every woman I sleep with!" he retorted on a thread of passionate humor.

"And I don't marry every man who claims he wants me in bed, either!"

"Waiting for love?" he taunted, lowering his head once again to her bared breast.

"Yes!"

His teeth closed around her nipple, sending a gasping wave of desire and helpless panic through her. She was fighting to recover from it when the second attack was launched. The rough fingers probing her thigh swooped, claiming the intimate warmth of her.

Dara moaned and twisted in reaction. She was shivering from the physical exertion of trying to maintain her control and from the effects of his lovemaking.

"I'm going to steal your soul, darling Dara," Yale growled raspingly as he tightened his hold. "Your warm, inviting body will come with it!"

"Yale, please!"

"Begging already? What happened to the fierce resolve?"

137

"Damn you!"

"Don't say that, honey," he ordered hoarsely. "Accept the truth. You want me. I want you. Let yourself go and see where it leads. . . ."

"I already know where it leads! To cheap motels and even cheaper love!"

"The surroundings don't matter! I've told you that!" he grated tersely and then punished her with his teeth.

She flinched at the small, sharp pain on her nipple and cried out softly. Instantly he relented, but his hand didn't cease its erotic pattern between her thighs. Dara felt the buildup of that strange, curling sensation in her stomach and wanted to shout her defiance of it and the man who caused it.

He felt her trembling against him and she knew his body responded to her weakness with the eagerness of the predator to the prey. Yes, she thought wildly, the *hunter*, wasn't that what he had called himself? She was being systematically hunted, forced to react to each new foray against her body.

But she had her own goal and she knew this wasn't the way to reach it.

"Stop fighting me, sweetheart," he urged. "Feel what your body is telling you. My God! It's almost screaming the message at me! How can I deny it? You're shivering with your need. You're moist and hot and shaking with it. How can you deny yourself?"

"I can, Yale," she whispered harshly. "When I've made up my mind, I can do anything. And the devil in you tonight can't change that!"

"The hunter in me tonight could take his quarry without too much effort, I think," he growled, letting his tongue taste the fine sheen of perspiration in the valley between her breasts.

"It would be rape, Yale. I swear to heaven, it would be rape! Because I'm not going to ask for it tonight!"

She felt the taut, muscular chest beneath her cheek,

knew the still-leashed power in him and wondered if he would force himself on her, after all. Was there anything of the Southern gentleman in him now?

"I don't want you to merely ask for it," he rasped. "I want you to *beg* for it!"

"You won't get that from me, not tonight!"

He moved, settling her back onto the pillows and leaned over her. His hands were planted on either side of her, caging her. In the darkness he was a demon in black with amber-colored hair and she knew the overwhelming dominance in him, knew he was barely restraining himself from taking what he'd come to think of as his.

"Perhaps not tonight, Dara, but how long can you hold out? How long can you deny both of us?"

"As long as I have to!" she vowed, lying very still, instinct telling her not to provoke him physically or she would be lost.

"What are you waiting for?" he demanded brutally. "That so-called normal relationship you mentioned? Don't you know there is no such thing? Not between us. It's too late!"

"I don't believe that!" Her head moved on the pillow, sending the deep fire of her hair out in a fan which caught his eye for an instant.

"You're waiting for the magic click, aren't you?" he accused suddenly. "How long did it take before you felt it with that other man? The one you mentioned at lunch?"

Dara stared at him and then drew a deep breath. "With him it happened the moment we met."

There was a shattering stillness as the hazel fires raged in his eyes for an uncontrolled instant. "For everyone's sake, make sure he and I never meet, Dara. I'll take him apart. Literally."

She sucked in her breath at the violence in him. In that instant she could well imagine the dangerous, uncivilized man he had been in the past. She had a sharp vision of him taking a knife to anyone who dared call him names, she could see him risking the dark mountain roads with his illegal cargo and she could visualize him taking part in a tavern brawl. The Southern-gentleman veneer was thin, indeed.

"Don't worry," she flung back hastily. "I'm not anxious for any more violent scenes!"

"What happened to that relationship?" he asked between clenched teeth.

"I told you at lunch, I don't want to discuss it!"

"You told a *gentleman* at lunch that you didn't want to talk about it. He had to accept the answer, but I don't! Tell me, Dara. What went wrong with the magic click the last time?"

She felt the seething tension in him, knew he was determined to have an answer, and she was at a loss as to what to say. It had been a mistake to let him think there had been someone else, someone who was perfect for her. . . .

"There were . . . are . . . complications."

"Complications! Are you implying it might not be completely over?" he asked incredulously.

"If we can get things worked out . . ." Dara hedged recklessly, wondering desperately if she was doing the right thing by goading him like this.

"Forget it!" he snarled. "Don't even *think* about him again, do you understand me? Whatever you had or didn't have, it's over and done with. It was finished the night you left that party with me! You aren't in love with him, you can't be in love with him. If you were in love with another man, there's no way on earth you could have given yourself to me the way you did this weekend!"

"How do you know?" she couldn't resist challenging. "You hardly know me at all. You can't begin to guess what I might or might not be capable of doing!"

He glared at her for an instant as if he couldn't understand her argument. "No," he said with appalling emphasis. "I know you well enough to be sure of that much. *You aren't in love with anyone else!*"

"Whatever you say, Yale," she tossed back recklessly.

"Remember that!" he rapped. "The safety of your charming neck may depend on it!"

"Don't threaten me!"

"Why not? You belong to me. I can threaten you as much as I please!"

"One weekend out of my life doesn't give you any rights!"

"The hell it doesn't," he gritted. "Where I come from, a man takes the rights he wants."

"You may be from those lawless mountains, but you don't live there anymore! You're supposed to be maintaining another life-style now."

"You have only yourself to blame for shattering that life-style. You should have let well enough alone, been content with the Southern-gentleman accountant. He might have given you the time you seem to want. But you had to go and dig up the other half of me. Now you've got all of me on your trail and you don't stand a chance."

"You won't find me a casual bed partner!" she vowed.

"You *will* surrender! You can't give yourself the way you did this weekend and then change your mind about the relationship because it didn't develop the way you wanted!"

"You sound as if you're the one who got used this past weekend!"

"I did! You used me and then you tried to drop me. But it won't work, Dara. You're not going to walk all over my pride and get away with it!"

"You're doing this because of your pride?" She gasped, horrified.

"That's part of it," he retorted chillingly. "I'm also doing it because I still want you! With motives like that, a man doesn't give up easily."

"But those aren't the motives I want from a man!" she cried.

"I know. You have a preconceived notion of how things should be between yourself and a lover, but things don't always go the way we think they should. You're mine, Dara, and I'm going to make you admit that. You're not going to walk away and go flitting off to someone else who fits your mental image of the proper sort of lover!"

He surged to his feet and stood for a moment beside the bed, hazel eyes roving her slightly crushed and wholly abandoned looking figure.

"Tomorrow night you'd better keep in mind that I'm determined to have you! Sooner or later I'll get you where you belong: in bed and pleading for more of what you discovered in that damn motel!"

Moving with the frightening grace of a leopard, the devil who had invaded Dara's bedroom disappeared.

9

It was like dealing with two different men, Dara thought a little hysterically the next evening when she met her civilized accountant at the door.

Once again Yale was all good manners, sober suit and charm. The only clue to the devil in him lay in the gleam of hazel eyes through the lenses of his glasses and the flash of gold in his smile.

Dara was ready for him in more ways than one. She flung open the door and hurled the accusation at him before he'd even managed to step across the threshold.

"You followed me to work this morning!"

He arched one amber brow in polite inquiry. "I don't think that was me," he offered. His eyes swept her sleekly parted burnt-russet hair, the sun-bright, long yellow dress which flowed over her full curves and the sparkling challenge in the gray-green eyes.

"Of course it was you! I couldn't mistake that car, and you know it! It was the same you who came prowling into my bedroom uninvited last night!"

143

"Like I said, it wasn't me. Not quite. What honest, Internal-Revenue-Service–fearing accountant would go around doing things like that?"

"You're going to stand there and deny you're . . . you're trailing me?" she snapped, dumbfounded. "Stop playing games, Yale."

"You really ought to take this up with him," Yale advised helpfully, lifting the shawl from the back of a nearby chair and placing it solicitously around her shoulders.

"I don't believe this," she gasped, whirling to stare at him in confusion and annoyance. "Stop pretending you're some sort of split personality!"

"Why not? Two hunters are much more effective than one. Come along, Dara, I've got reservations in half an hour."

"Yale," she protested weakly, uncertain how to handle the bizarre situation. A part of her found it vastly intriguing in spite of the danger she felt. "Yale," she went on determinedly, allowing him to guide her out to the car, "this is ridiculous!"

"I agree. You can call it off any time you wish," he informed her lightly as she slid into the leather interior.

"*I* can call it off! You're the one who's behaving in such a crazy fashion! They put people in straitjackets for this sort of thing!"

"Let's hope you don't let it go that far," he growled feelingly, starting the engine. "In the meantime, would you mind if we didn't talk about *him*? This is my evening and I'd prefer to have your full attention."

She caught the hopeful, whimsical note in his gently accented words and stared at him in a combination of disgust and amusement.

"Don't tell me you're jealous of . . . of that hunter who was in my room last night!" she dared.

He flashed her a slanting, enigmatic glance. "Why not?

He's had memories all day long of how you felt in his arms last night. As a proper Southern gentleman, I couldn't have barged into your bedroom without being invited. Is it any wonder?"

"Why should it bother you?" she demanded tartly. "You had the same memories!"

"This could get confusing, couldn't it?" He chuckled warmly, downshifting for a light.

"Does that mean you'll give up this crazy charade?" she said quickly.

"No, but let's talk about something besides me," he retorted easily. "Tonight you're on a date with a man whose manners you can rely on implicitly. Why not enjoy it? Have all those conversations you wanted to have that make you think we're developing a normal relationship."

"Are you making fun of me?" she muttered suspiciously.

"A gentleman never makes fun of a lady," he intoned piously.

It took a violent effort of will for Dara to stifle the laughter which threatened to bubble over inside her. As it was, the humor was clear in her eyes although she managed to keep her expression suitably haughty.

"And you, of course, are the perfect gentleman. Forgive me. I don't know how I could have made such an accusation. You'll have to understand, I've had a rather upsetting few days," she murmured with social apology.

"I'm sorry to hear that," he returned commiseratingly. "Life is full of the unexpected, though, isn't it?"

"Yes, but those with fortitude and endurance can cope."

"You have both?"

"Definitely!"

"Excellent. How did work go today? Did you put together the information on those securities you mentioned?" he asked politely.

"Yes. I have it at home, as a matter of fact. Remind me tonight and I'll give it to you." She eyed him coolly, assessing her decision to treat him exactly as he wished.

"What else are you following besides electronics? I want to keep the portfolio diversified," he began conversationally.

"Some of the new medical-research stocks may be good but very risky. The new emphasis on gene technology is bound to revolutionize the field, but a lot of starters are going to get left behind in the dust," she mused.

"I don't mind some high-risk stuff. I've got enough of the blue chips as it is," he told her easily, pulling into the parking lot of the restaurant he'd selected.

"Just how gutsy do you feel?" she asked challengingly.

"Whenever a stockbroker gets that particular gleam in her eyes I get nervous," he said, parking the Alfa Romeo with second-nature precision. "What are we going to short?"

"How did you guess?" She grinned.

"I've been burned on one short sale," he warned her, assisting her out of the car with male grace. "It would have to be a very, very sure thing. . . ."

"There is no such animal as a 'sure thing'!"

He sighed. "Tell me about it."

"Well, there's this small computer company which got caught up in the run-up of technology stocks last year. But I happen to know they're on very shaky gound now. Their financial base is practically nonexistent. It can't be long before the market realizes just how precariously balanced the firm is," she said enthusiastically as they were shown to their seats.

"You enjoy your work, don't you?" Yale smiled, sitting down across from her and scanning her eager, excited face with amused interest.

"Love it. Knew I would the first day on the job! All the challenge and excitement and thrills . . ." She shrugged self-deprecatingly. "There's nothing quite like the day-to-day highs and lows of the securities business."

"So tell me more about this little computer company you're proposing to short," he murmured.

"The stock is almost bound to go down, and soon," she confided, leaning forward intently. "As a matter of fact, I'm going to short it in my own portfolio."

"You manage your own account?"

"Naturally. I don't intend making all those profits for other folks and not taking some of the benefits for myself!"

"So you're proposing we borrow some of this computer firm's stock, sell it while it's high and then buy it back when it tumbles. Our profit being the difference," he clarified, picking up the tasseled menu.

"A lot of people forget there's money to be made on a stock that's going down as well as on a stock that's going up," Dara reminded him.

"There's a hell of a lot more risk involved selling a stock short," he grumbled. "Ask me—I know!"

"How badly were you burned?" she asked sympathetically.

"I panicked when the stock which was guaranteed to tumble started going up a point a day!"

She winced. "How many days before you bailed out and took the loss?"

"Ten," he told her wryly. "I lost about five thousand."

"Oh, dear. I suppose you're really not interested in trying another short sale, then?"

"A gentleman can nearly always be talked into anything by a woman he'd like to seduce." Yale grinned, glancing up from the menu with a deliberately sardonic expression in his eyes.

"I'll keep that in mind," she managed to fling back spiritedly.

The evening passed with surprising swiftness, the

conversation moving quickly from one topic to another. Dara was astounded to realize hours later on the drive home that she had almost forgotten about the strange game Yale was playing. She was too involved in getting to know her Southern gentleman better and in getting him to know her.

She was floating on a contented haze created by what she told herself was the success of the evening when they reached her front door. Smiling, she turned on the step.

"Would you like to come in for a brandy?"

"Yes." He smiled back. "I would."

She hesitated briefly as he took the key from her hand and inserted it in the lock.

"You will remember which role you're playing tonight, won't you?" she drawled in liquid tones.

"I'm still able to keep it straight," he assured her softly as she slipped past him to enter the apartment. "I'm hoping you'll let the two aspects of my personality reunite before any lasting damage is done to my psyche!"

Dara eased the shawl from her shoulders and knew a moment's inexplicable pleasure as his hand reached out to assist her, touching her nape lightly in the process.

"I refuse to take the blame for this double life you're intent on leading," she informed him coolly, walking toward the kitchen to get the brandy.

"You caused it."

He followed her, coming to lean negligently in the doorway as she went about the small domestic business. She could feel his eyes on her every move and determinedly refused to let it affect her.

"Do you suppose there was someone around when Pandora opened her box? Someone who forever after kept telling her that everything that happened was her fault?" She sighed.

"Probably," Yale said idly. "But, then, she deserved it."

"A woman can't help her natural curiosity." Dara

handed him the snifter and led the way back out into the cozy living room.

"Then she should learn to live with the consequences."

"What a pompous thing to say," she chided, sinking gracefully into a far corner of the sofa. The yellow skirts of her dress flared around her.

"Accountants sometimes seem a little pompous," he apologized, lowering himself casually across from her.

"*Men* sometimes seem a little pompous!" she corrected firmly.

"Whatever you say, ma'am," he drawled, his eyes laughing at her as he lifted his brandy glass.

"Now, there's a proper gentlemanly attitude. The lady is always right," Dara teased, inhaling the aromatic fumes trapped in the bell of the glass.

"Or else she's afraid," he added agreeably, sipping his drink.

"Afraid!"

Dara stared at him, the lighthearted teasing dying in her eyes.

"Umm," he confirmed as if he hadn't noticed her sudden irritation. "What else can I call it when, having opened the box, Pandora tries very hard to shut it again, even though she liked what she found inside?"

"Caution! Common sense! Intelligence!"

"All good qualities in a stockbroker, but when they appear in the woman behind the broker, one has to ask why."

"Yale, what exactly are you trying to say? Do you think you can talk me into bed by calling me a coward?" Dara's eyebrows drew together in warning.

"No, I'm only trying to understand your actions. The only way they make any sense is if we accept the fact that there's a measure of cowardice involved here." He smiled at her in a lofty way that irked Dara.

"You might be feeling a little cowardly yourself if you

found yourself the victim of a . . . a two-pronged hunt!"
she gritted, swallowing a larger part of the brandy.

"No, that won't serve as an excuse," he told her softly,
leaning back against the cushions and stretching out his
legs contentedly while he considered the problem. "You
can cope with both pursuers if you wish." He turned his
head to look at her searchingly. "Tell me the truth,
honey: Why are you trying to back off from the relationship we began this past weekend?"

"I've told you, Yale. I want a normal, properly developed one. I never meant to wind up in bed with you that
first night, and you know it. It got everything off on the
wrong foot," she said, speaking into her snifter.

"Maybe things between us didn't start out following
the acceptable pattern, but that doesn't mean they're not
right . . ." he started earnestly, breaking off when she
flung up her head, brilliant eyes almost pure green.

"I let myself get rushed into a whirlwind relationship
once before, and it was a disaster! I'm not going to let it
happen again, and that's final! This time it will go along a
reasonable, natural path, or it won't go at all!"

For a few assessing seconds he watched her, studying
the grim resolution in her set face.

"Your marriage?" he hazarded coolly. "Or this other
man?"

"What other man?" she clipped.

"The one you told me about last night," he said dryly.

"Oh, him." She bent over her brandy, swirling it
carefully in the bottom of the glass. "I was . . . was
referring to my marriage," she confessed at last, surprised at herself. She had never told anyone about the
fears which had haunted her since that early mistake.

"Tell me about it," he whispered persuasively, putting
out a hand to trail soothing fingers down the length of her
yellow sleeve. "You said he was charming, kind, that you
had a lot in common, but that you never felt the
click. . . ."

"It was all a long time ago, Yale. I told you, I hardly ever think about it anymore. I'm not bitter, just cautious."

"He rushed you off your feet? Pushed you into marriage and then, six months later, admitted he'd changed his mind?"

"That's it in a nutshell." She shrugged. "Not his fault or anyone else's except, possibly, mine for not slowing things down and letting the relationship develop more before committing myself."

"Your fault!" he muttered harshly. "How can you blame yourself? My God, woman! He used you! Can't you see that? How old were you at the time?"

"He didn't . . . At least, he never meant . . . I was twenty-two," she finished lamely.

"And how old was he?"

"Thirty-one."

"That settles it," Yale bit out succinctly. "You were used. He was old enough to have more integrity than to sweep a young woman off her feet and marry her just to punish his ex-fiancée! And you've spent the last eight years somehow thinking the disaster was all your fault, haven't you?"

She drew a deep breath. "I had six months, Yale, and I couldn't make it work. It started going downhill from day one. If I'd demanded that we get to know each other better before the marriage, not let him talk me into it until we'd developed our relationship into something besides a romance, it all could have been avoided. I would have learned about the ex-fiancée and, perhaps, understood what he was going through. . . ."

"That's garbage," Yale informed her with complete assurance. "And if I ever meet the guy, I'll flatten him. Not for divorcing you—I'm grateful to him for that—but for leaving you saddled with this ridiculous guilt and fear!"

"You're starting to sound like your other half!" she managed flippantly, wondering how she'd ever let the conversation veer off into this particular channel. It was a channel which had been closed for a long, long time.

"Sorry, but even we accountants have our limits!"

"Yale," she began placatingly, not quite knowing what to say next.

"Sweetheart, I know what I'm talking about. I know what it means to be used. I know what it means to be married for an ulterior motive!"

"Did you love her very much?" Dara breathed, thinking of the young woman he had brought out of the hills with him.

"No," he said quietly, his eyes on the unicorn tapestry as if the truth were woven into it. "She was a pretty little thing and I was attracted to her. We'd known each other all our lives. I guess I felt some sort of responsibility to take her with me when I left the mountains. She wanted out as much as I did. I knew exactly how she was feeling and I couldn't leave her behind. We had everything in common, you'll have to grant us that," he said sardonically. "We knew everything there was to know about each other. And it still wasn't enough to save the marriage."

There was a short silence.

"Is that why you mock my efforts to build a more solid relationship before we go back to bed?" she prodded in a surprisingly steady voice. "You don't have any faith in my approach?"

He shook his head slowly. "What I'm saying is that time and propinquity won't make much difference if two people simply aren't right for each other to begin with. As for the argument of getting to know each other well before the relationship moves to the bedroom, I don't have any problems with that—"

Dara interrupted with a quick, grateful smile. "Then you *do* understand something of what I'm trying to say!"

He eyed her consideringly. "I was about to say that in

our case, we didn't violate your strictures the way you seem to think we did!"

"What are you talking about? We hardly knew each other a few hours before we found ourselves in that . . . that sleazy motel room!"

"Don't call it sleazy," he said with a lazy grin. "I have very pleasant thoughts of that motel room. What I meant was, even though we only spent a few hours together before we checked into that motel, we knew an awful lot about each other. You knew more about me by that time than you knew about your first husband when you married him!"

"Well, you didn't know much about me! The next morning you were convinced I'd gone to bed with you in order to secure your stock account!" she retorted icily. "And the next night you were willing to pay an even higher price! In both cases you acted as if you were involved in a business transaction!"

He set his snifter down on the glass table and reached to remove hers from her fingers. "Doesn't the fact that I was willing to pay any price you asked tell you something important?" he whispered, pulling her gently, coaxingly into his arms.

"It tells me you may not be a very good businessman!" she attempted bravely as his hands closed around her.

"Think what a fortune in commissions you'll make off me! I'll probably wind up buying any off-the-wall stock you pitch at me!"

He cut off any retort she might have made by sealing her mouth with his. The tip of his tongue probed persuasively at the gate of her fiercely clenched lips and his fingers began working their way suggestively down her spine to her waist.

"Oh, Yale," Dara murmured and heard his pleased masculine chuckle. An instant later he had gained the territory of her mouth. She gave in to the heated call of his body, nestling into the curve of his arm.

The intoxicating male scent of him was like a drug on her senses, senses that had already been seduced by an evening of tantalizing conversation and the undeniable excitement a woman feels in the presence of a man who wants her. She felt him free a hand to remove his glasses.

Telling herself that Yale in his Southern-gentleman role would be much easier to handle when the time came to say good night, Dara allowed herself to be drawn closer to the flame. Her cheek moved luxuriously against the roughness of his jacket as her head rested on his shoulder. Everything about this man elicited a response from her senses. Everything clicked.

"You have a way of feeding the fire in me even when you're sitting across the table trying to sell securities to me!" Yale's muttered accusation was heavy with undisguised desire.

His hands tightened in the thickness of her hair, holding her unmercifully still while he drank his fill of her lips.

"Touch me, Dara," he commanded huskily as her fingers crept up the front of his jacket and found the buttons of his shirt. "I love to feel your hands on me. You do want me, sweetheart. Admit that much, at least!"

"I want you, Yale," she whispered, eyes closing in utter pleasure as he lifted the hair aside and found her throat with his lips. "You must know that!"

"I know it," he growled against the skin of her shoulder. "I just want to make sure you do."

She felt a vague trickle of alarm stir at the back of her mind.

"Why?" she pleaded starkly.

"Because it will make it easier for you to tell that other man he has to go!"

She felt the abrupt tension in him as he pushed her slowly back against the cushions. Simultaneously he lowered the zipper of the yellow gown, and by the time

154

she found herself beneath him, the bodice had been lowered to her waist.

Mutely she watched as he raised himself far enough away to shrug out of the jacket, flinging it aside, and then he was covering her again. His hands glided down her throat to her breasts and his legs settled with arrogant force between her thighs. The yellow skirt was hiked up almost to her hips and Dara felt ravished.

"You must tell him soon, Dara," he grated, dusting the valley between her breasts with tiny, stinging little kisses. "Tomorrow. Get rid of him!"

"Yale, let me explain," she begged, arching instinctively into his body.

"No. I don't want to talk about him anymore. Just tell him it's over. Tell him on the phone. I don't want you seeing him again," he rasped.

"You're starting to sound like your other self again," she told him tauntingly, filled suddenly with an inexplicable desire to goad and provoke. He made her go a little crazy when he did this to her, she realized. And the notion of his being jealous was satisfying, indeed. Even if it was terribly risky.

"The two of us are perfectly in accord when it comes to some things," Yale vowed, sliding slowly down her body. "We share a common goal, remember!"

"Oh!"

The exclamation was torn from her as his hands, moving forcefully down her ribs and waist, pushed the soft yellow fabric over her hips. His tongue went over her skin with a damp heat that made her writhe and her fingers clench fiercely in the amber of his hair.

"Oh, Yale!"

Her mounting excitement seemed to inflame him further and his lips teased at her waist and stomach. She moaned, her head tossing restlessly on the cushion, and tried to gain some semblance of control over her spinning senses. Desperately she made herself think of the previous night and how she had sworn she would not invite him to her bed again. Not until she was sure of him. . . .

"You will tell him in the morning, won't you, Dara?"

"Tell who . . . what . . . ?" It was becoming impossible to think, she realized. She had to get a grip on her emotions. It was too soon. She couldn't give in, not yet, not with so much at stake. . . .

"That other man, damn it!" he said harshly, his teeth nipping with deliberate punishment at her vulnerable inner thigh. She flinched, and instantly his tongue came out to soothe the spot.

"There won't be any other man in your life except me! You're building a relationship with me, no one else! Is that understood?"

"Yes," she breathed, "Yes, Yale, I understand. There won't be anyone else. . . ." As long as you're around, there couldn't be anyone else, don't you know that? she added silently.

"Good," he said with such complete satisfaction that he gave himself away. Dara sucked in her breath in sudden, overpowering fury.

"Why, you . . . you bas—" She broke off of her own accord, knowing that even in the heat of her anger, she couldn't fling that particular word at him again. "You arrogant, overbearing, domineering, *trucker!* What makes you think you can make love to me until I'll do whatever you want?"

"Wait," he protested as her fingers tightened threateningly in his hair. She could feel the rueful laughter in him and tugged harder. "Wait, honey, that can't be me you're describing!"

"Don't give me that, you wolf in accountant's clothing! I'll teach you to try and seduce me!"

She began to struggle free of him, kicking at his leg with her sandaled foot and yanking unmercifully on the amber hair. How dare he play that game with her tonight? How dare he ruin her wonderful evening!

Yale must have realized she was beyond reasoning. He moved quickly, efficiently, grabbing her wrists and chaining them in one firm fist. He used the sheer force of his weight and strength to stifle her twisting, scrabbling efforts to be free.

He didn't hurt her, but he bore down on her, crushing her so completely into the cushions that she couldn't move. There he let her futilely struggle until she had exhausted herself.

"Damn you!" she seethed, infuriated at his patience while he waited for her to calm down. "You are the most annoying man I have ever met! And you were supposed to be a gentleman tonight!" she ended on a wail.

"I *am* behaving like a gentleman," he told her bluntly, hazel eyes hardening as he met her furious glare. "And you, my vicious little tabby, ought to be grateful at the moment! There are several very *ungentlemanly* things I'd like to do to you right now!"

"What's stopping you?" she demanded recklessly.

"The knowledge that I deserved the attack, I guess," he admitted with an abrupt, rueful little grin. "I was using a rather underhanded method to achieve my goal, wasn't I?"

"You certainly were!" she assured him fervently, her nearly green eyes narrowing. "And don't think this boyish, abashed little apology is going to make everything all right! It's time for my *gentleman* friend to leave!"

"Kicking me out again?" he asked sadly.

"With pleasure!"

He sighed, sitting up and releasing her carefully. Hastily she tugged the dress back up to her shoulders, aware of his mocking scrutiny.

"I meant it, you know," he said softly as she scrambled to a sitting position at the far end of the couch.

"Meant what?" she grumbled, trying to pull the zipper up far enough to hold the dress in place. She refused to look at him.

"Get rid of him, Dara."

She shivered suddenly at the cold intent in his words and her teeth unconsciously caught her lower lip in a small gesture of wariness as she turned her head to look at him.

"You and I have enough to do settling the matter of this relationship of ours. I won't have another man involved."

She stared at him for a long moment, aware of the strength of his will. She could feel the force of it flowing around her, binding her, defying her to ignore it. How jealous was he? Did his jealousy indicate love or was it merely an instinctive possessiveness toward a woman he happened to find himself wanting?

"It seems to me," she drawled with amazing daring, "that if I give up this 'other' man, the odds become rather poor."

"What's that supposed to mean?" he demanded roughly, picking up his glasses and putting them on with an impatient gesture.

"It becomes a case of two against one," she mocked, "Both of you against me. . . ."

"That strikes me as just about even!"

"Yale!"

"Dara," he said with such quiet menace that she was positive both the devil and the gentleman were totally united for the moment. "This is not a negotiable point. Get rid of him!"

He snagged her wrist before she could answer, got to his feet and pulled her up beside him. "Give me your word that there won't be any other men involved, or I'll give you mine that I won't leave tonight until I have your promise!"

Locked to him by the savage grip on her wrist, Dara

stared up at him, wide-eyed and knowing this was one way of playing the game that wouldn't work.

"There won't be another man in my life, Yale," she capitulated with a submissiveness that appalled her. But, then, she acknowledged to herself, it was nothing less than the truth.

10

After he had extracted her promise to get rid of the nonexistent other man, Yale's hunting settled into a clear, dangerous pattern. Dara was helplessly intrigued by the novelty of being seduced by two men in the same body. She was also very much afraid at times that she would go crazy.

Her responses to the Southern gentleman and his alter ego were amusingly different and, she told herself ruefully, equally intense. With her accountant there were pleasant luncheons and evenings spent in conversation on a variety of subjects. They argued about the stock market, with Yale losing. He, in turn, talked of tax shelters and clever accounting strategies. They discussed mutual interests in books, films and politics.

"You know," he told her over a sinfully rich dessert of Burnt Cream which Dara had prepared one evening, "you have what used to be called a Renaissance mind. No matter what we talk about, you seem to have some information on the subject!"

"No." She smiled, scooping up a spoonful of the luscious dessert. "I'm a dabbler. People with Renaissance minds are supposed to be accomplished in all their interests. I just dabble around until I find the ones that . . ."

"Click?" he provided wryly, slanting her an enigmatic glance.

"I'm afraid so," she admitted with an elegant little shrug.

The other advantage to the Southern gentleman, Dara told herself time and again as she was bid good night, was that he really did behave like a gentleman. There were no more awkward scenes or threatened seductions when she would deliberately draw the evening to a close. It wasn't that Yale didn't kiss her with passion and a clear desire to carry matters into the bedroom; he did. But he took his dismissals with grace, and Dara knew that if the lovemaking ever went further it would be entirely her own fault.

The times spent with her gentleman accountant were civilized, casually sophisticated and delightful for Dara. She loved this side of Yale. She could relax with this man. Relax and enjoy herself while working on the construction of a relationship that, she told herself, had a lasting basis.

The word *relax* was the antonym of what she felt when the hunting devil from the hills appeared. Dara never had any trouble telling the two men apart. Yale made no effort to blunt the sensual menace which seemed to radiate from him when he chose to pursue her in this guise.

He set her nerves on edge whenever he was in the vicinity. Glancing into her rearview mirror and finding the Alfa Romeo following her to work or parked in the lot outside a store in which she had been shopping was enough to send chills down her spine.

He had the audacity to show up on her doorstep one

night after she had gone to bed, leaning on the doorbell until she finally answered.

"To whom do I have the pleasure of speaking?" she'd demanded caustically when she'd finally dragged herself out of bed, flung on her fluffy robe and padded to the front door. The question was rhetorical. She'd known at once.

"Guess," Yale had suggested with his wicked smile.

She'd studied his negligent pose in the doorjamb with the wary, narrowed green gaze this version of Yale always elicited.

"I sent you home three hours ago," Dara had tried tartly, already aware of the excitement fluttering from her head to her toes.

"You sent *him* home," he'd corrected, sliding a foot over the threshold and gently forcing her back into the wall. "Me, I'm just getting started for the evening."

He had been dressed all in black again, the amber hair slightly ruffled, the glasses nowhere in evidence. Dara had instinctively clutched the robe more tightly around herself and sought for a way to deal with the dangerous situation.

"That's far enough, Yale. I want you to leave."

"Show me," he invited, clamping his strong hands around her shoulders and pulling her forcibly against the lean darkness of him. "Show me how badly you want me to leave!"

It had taken an extraordinary effort of willpower and Dara had found herself precariously close to surrender before she had managed the feat, but at last she had sent the devil away. His rage and frustration had been clearly evident, and the roar of the Alfa Romeo had been alarming as it disappeared in the distance.

Dara had leaned against the wall, regrouping her forces after the onslaught, and wondered how much longer she could survive the perilous game.

But the next day the gentleman was back, acting as if

nothing at all had happened since he had wined and dined her so beguilingly the previous evening. Dara had given up berating him for the actions of his other half. Yale simply pretended a total lack of interest in the subject. She had drawn a long sigh of relief and relaxed once more.

The week slipped by rapidly, and by its end Dara was doing her best to see as much of the gentleman and as little of the devil as she could. Feeling a bit silly, she issued an invitation to the accountant. At least Yale was consistent in his personalities. Invitations made to the accountant were accepted by him. He didn't switch roles on her unexpectedly. It gave Dara a certain reassurance for which she was increasingly grateful.

"A picnic?" he repeated, sounding pleased. "That sounds interesting. What shall I bring?"

"Whatever will fit in a bike pouch." Dara chuckled. It was Friday night and she was once again bidding him farewell on her doorstep. "You do have a bike, don't you?"

"No, but I know where I can borrow one," he offered smilingly.

"Hmm. That won't do around here, you know. You'll have to get one of your own if you're going to become a genuine Eugene resident."

"Yes, ma'am," he agreed humbly.

She was carefully arranging the last of the sandwiches in her large bike bag late the next morning when he appeared. She turned at the hiss of tires on the sidewalk and found him dressed in jeans, mounted on a racy-looking red ten-speed. The collar of his brown pullover was open.

"You must have a very friendly neighbor! That's an expensive bike!" she said, admiring the lines.

He patted the low-slung handlebars. "My paperboy. He let me have it this morning after he finished his run. Nice kid."

She watched him swing lithely off the bike and push it over to where she puttered around her own yellow steed.

"You sure you wouldn't rather take the car?" he asked dubiously as she finished her preparations. His eyes scanned her tight-fitting jeans and open-necked green shirt.

The dark hunter would have reached out to pat the luxurious roundness of her derriere and the hazel eyes would have rested appreciatively on the full curve of her breast, but the gentleman was much more polite. Yale's smiling gaze warmed but he said nothing.

"Oh, no, this is a perfect day for a bike ride," she assured him, strapping the bag shut and mounting with practiced ease. "Ready?"

"Lead the way," he invited.

It was a delight to the senses to be whisking through the warm sunlight of an Oregon morning with the man she loved by her side, Dara thought blissfully. The bikes sailed over the road and the wind whistled past her ears.

"The river?" Yale asked, turning his head to glance at her laughing profile.

"I know a perfect spot." She grinned.

She led him through the wooded five-hundred-acre park, past the five-mile jogging trail and a long canal designed for canoeing, into a quiet landscape of green fields and tall trees.

"This is good country," Yale murmured quietly.

"The best," Dara agreed with the deep pleasure of the native Oregonian.

"I hadn't realized how important the Willamette River Valley was to the history of the settlement of the West," Yale mused reflectively.

Dara winced at his pronunciation of the river's name. "In addition to getting a bike, you'd better learn how to pronounce the name of the river." She chuckled. "It's Wil-LAMB-it. And you're right. This river was as much an influence on this region as the Mississippi and Ohio rivers were on their states. We used to have steamboats on it transporting the cargo between the different towns. People coming from back East thought they'd found heaven when they finally reached the Willamette Valley."

"I know how they felt," Yale said gently, flicking her an amused glance.

Warmed by the look in his eyes, Dara pretended to be busy searching for a suitable picnic spot.

"How does this look?" she suggested, indicating an isolated woodsy area.

"Fine," he agreed, gliding the bike to a halt. "But let's go a little farther from the path. I don't like spectators when I eat."

"Sorry I couldn't stuff a blanket into the pack," Dara apologized as they led the bikes off the trail and located a grassy spot on which to sit.

"That's what jeans are for," Yale said lightly, glancing around as if to assure himself of a reasonable measure of privacy. Then he bent over to fumble with his own bike bag.

"What did you bring?" Dara demanded interestedly as she withdrew the sandwiches, fruit and cookies from her own pack.

He produced a half-liter bottle of Burgundy, and she grinned approvingly.

"I even remembered a couple of paper cups," he told her virtuously, coming to sit down beside her on the grass.

"The perfect date," Dara said sweetly, opening sandwiches.

"I try."

"The other Yale could take a few lessons from you," she noted, not looking at him.

"I don't really feel like talking about him at the moment," Yale said smoothly, reaching eagerly for the nearest sandwich. "What have I got here?"

"Salmon and capers," she told him. "There's also one

with a butter spread of dried herbs and wine and a chutney and cheese mixture."

"No tuna fish or ham and cheese?" he mocked, surveying the cleverly cut sandwiches with enthusiasm.

"I've decided it's time you expanded your food horizons," she retorted condescendingly. "Every time we go out you order steak-and-potatoes-type meals."

"I'm willing to learn. I always feel like I'm indulging my senses when I'm around you," he added meaningfully.

Dara flushed and took an industrious bite out of her sandwich while Yale calmly uncorked the wine.

"I've been doing some serious thinking about this streak of cowardice in you," he went on conversationally as he poured the Burgundy into the paper cups.

Dara nearly choked on her sandwich.

"Cowardice!" she managed, gasping for air.

"That's what it amounts to, I think." Yale nodded thoughtfully, slapping her helpfully between the shoulders. "Why else would you have backed off from where we had gone with this relationship of ours?"

"Yale, we've been through this," she began firmly.

"I realize that, but I'm starting to get worried," he explained patiently.

"Worried! What about, for heaven's sake!"

"You've implied you're waiting for the magic 'click.' What I'm wondering about is, how will you know it when it occurs? What are the signs? Are you just going to turn to me someday and say, "'Okay, Yale, it happened'?"

"Hardly!" She sniffed. How could she explain it had already happened?

"Then how am I going to know when you've come to your senses and realized you want this relationship as much as I do?" he pressed gently, his expression one of genuine, studious concern.

"Relationships should evolve over a period of time, Yale."

166

"Time can be telescoped under the right circumstances," he said quietly.

"Perhaps," she agreed carefully. "But it didn't happen like that in our case, did it? Our relationship didn't exactly take place in the right circumstances!"

"Are you going to hold that motel room against me forever?"

"Maybe," Dara declared. "It sure got us off to a bad start!"

"What about the next night, Dara? Why did you withdraw your demand that I marry you?"

"No woman wants to force a man into marriage!" she snapped, gulping a swallow of the wine.

"I was willing. . . ."

"To pay a price. That's hardly calculated to convince a woman of undying love!"

"You never asked for my undying love," he pointed out softly.

Dara felt the red wash into her cheeks and glanced away from the intent hazel eyes.

"You made it very clear the next morning that your demand for marriage had merely been a means of trying to stop me from seducing you," he went on after a moment. "You withdrew it because it hadn't worked. And now you're using every other means at your disposal to keep from winding up in bed with me again. Why is that, honey?"

"Must you be deliberately obtuse?" she gritted. "I'm trying to let a normal relationship develop. How many times do I have to tell you? I want to be sure."

"There are no certainties in this life, Dara. You can't positively protect yourself against making the kind of mistake you made with your first husband. Sometimes you have to take a risk."

"I disagree," she said staunchly, glad it was the gentleman who was having this argument with her and not the devil. "I think one can take steps to ensure that things are right between two people!"

"Which brings me back to my initial question," he interrupted. "How will you know? How will I know you've finally made the big discovery?"

Dara was at a loss. There was no way to tell him she'd already made her discovery and was merely waiting for him to make his. He would either fall in love with her or he wouldn't.

"I expect one knows when one is in love," she evaded coolly.

"Ah," he breathed, "is that what you're waiting for? To fall in love?"

"I don't want a relationship based on . . . on sex, Yale. You must understand that. If that's all we have together, then—"

"Then you're going to break it off and go your own way, is that it?" he growled.

She shrugged helplessly. "I suppose that's the way it will have to be."

There was a tight pause. "How long did you know your first husband before you married him?" he finally asked.

"A . . . a few weeks," she confessed. "I told you, it was a whirlwind courtship. We were married less than four weeks after we met. He was eager to get on with it, I suppose, because his ex-fiancée had already married. . . ."

"And how long would you have had to know him to realize it wasn't going to work? To realize you were allowing yourself to be used?" Yale probed.

Dara sighed. Resting her arms on her drawn-up knees, she gazed out over the wooded countryside. "I don't know. Perhaps a few months. . . ."

"A few months!" he exclaimed, his irritation seeping through the gentlemanly exterior. "How many months? Six? ten? How many?"

"In that case, I suppose three or four would have done it," she admitted, remembering how long it had taken before she realized another woman had a hold on her husband. An unbreakable hold.

"Four months," he repeated to himself. "Is that what you're proposing for us? A four-month period of getting to know each other thoroughly before we take up where we left off last weekend?"

"Is that too much to ask?" she flung back, suddenly annoyed. The burnt-russet sweep of her hair whipped about her neck as she snapped her head around to fix him with accusing gray-green eyes.

He met her gaze for an instant, and she swallowed unconsciously when she thought she saw a flash of the other Yale in his level stare. And then he looked away.

"Dara," he finally said quietly, absently shredding a blade of grass as he propped himself on one elbow and focused on the middle distance. "Are you sure you're not trying to punish both of us for what happened last weekend?"

"Of course I'm sure!"

"You said that first morning you would have your revenge," he reminded her.

"I was in a temper," she returned carelessly. "I didn't mean it." And it was true. Caution, fear, wariness, despair, all of those emotions had played a part in her subsequent actions, but not revenge. "I . . . I let myself wind up in bed with you again the next night, didn't I? If I had been bent on revenge that would hardly have happened!"

"I'm not so sure about that. You may not have been able to resist. . . ."

"That's ridiculous. Pure male ego talking!"

"We have something special together, honey," he murmured. "It wasn't until the second morning we woke up in each other's arms that you erected the wall. Practically your first words were to withdraw your marriage demand, and then you kicked me out of the apartment."

"But I wasn't in a flaming rage," she reminded him virtuously. "That time I acted in a rational, clearheaded fashion. No dire threats. That's when I'm at my most dangerous, Yale, when I'm thinking!"

"I see," he drawled, a trace of humor lacing his words. "And what you were thinking was that by the second time around you still hadn't felt this mysterious click, right? You still weren't sure of your feelings for me, so you decided to institute a trial period of getting to know each other."

"We need that time, Yale," she replied steadily.

"I don't think so," he returned almost casually. "I think you felt the magic in my arms and then tried to deny it in the morning. Maybe you're as much two different people right now as I am!"

"Nonsense!"

It was time to put an end to this threatening discussion, Dara decided firmly. She began picking up the sandwich wrappers and paper cups with a determined air.

"Time to get going," she told him lightly. "There's a long ride ahead of us before we get home!"

"Are you trying to exhaust me?" he demanded, the amusement in him telling her he was accepting the end of the picnic with good grace.

"That doesn't sound like a bad tactic. Maybe it would keep your alter ego from making late-night appearances in my bedroom!"

"Don't count on it. He's got a lot of stamina where you're concerned." He helped her with the trash, stowing part of it in his bike pouch until they could find a waste can.

It wasn't until they arrived at her apartment that he issued the invitation.

"Dara, will you have dinner with me tonight? At my

place?" he asked politely as they braked to a halt in her drive.

She hopped off the bike and glanced at him warily. "Who's issuing the invitation?"

"A gentleman and an accountant," he intoned righteously. "The Yale you seem to trust."

"Oh, I trust both Yales." She grinned rashly. "It's just that the other one is a little harder to handle! But I can always predict how he'll act, so, in a way, he's perfectly trustworthy!"

"But you wouldn't accept a dinner date with him?"

"Nope. But I will with the Southern gentleman. What time?"

"I'll pick you up at six."

"I can take my own car," she protested automatically.

"I wouldn't think of it. I'm issuing the invitation and I'll pick you up."

"A gentleman to the fingertips." She chuckled admiringly.

11

Dara dressed with absent care for the evening, her mind on Yale. It was not the first time she had been to his modern, multiwindowed condominium near the river. She had teased him that first time, telling him it was exactly the proper setting for a bachelor accountant.

The visit had occurred earlier in the week and had been surprisingly short. Yale had taken her home for an after-dinner drink. She could still remember how he'd stood in the living room, a glass in each hand, and watched broodingly as she wandered around with undisguised curiosity. The liqueur had been rushed down her throat and she had then been politely rushed home. No explanations.

Yale's home had reflected the image he seemed intent on projecting. As she adjusted the zipper of the black, knee-length dress, Dara thought of the carefully modern leather furniture, the too-appropriate accessories and paintings and the expensive quality throughout.

It had all been very masculine and in very good taste.

Nothing jabbed the eye or seemed obtrusive. Compared to her own rather eclectic decor, Yale's home was like a study out of a conservative home-and-garden magazine. He wanted it clear he had left the hills far behind. Dara smiled to herself. After they were married, she'd shake the place up a bit. It needed it!

Married! She scolded herself. She shouldn't be counting her chickens before they were hatched, damn it! A lot of time was still needed and a lot could still happen. . . .

She broke off the chiding thought, the narrow, kicky pleats in her skirt floating around her knees as she went to answer the doorbell.

"Hello, Yale." She smiled, the impact of him hitting her senses with the usual force. Did a woman always react this way to the mere sight of the man she loved on her doorstep?

"Ready?" He grinned, the gold flashing briefly. "You look lovely."

Behind the polite barrier of his glasses the hazel eyes skimmed the scoop-necked dress approvingly and then lifted to the sleekness of her simply styled hair. It was all very subtly done, but the message was clear. He liked what he saw. Dara warmed under the quiet caress.

"Thank you," she said softly, thinking that he seemed incredibly attractive to her no matter what he wore. Tonight the dark slacks emphasized the lean power of his build and the properly buttoned white shirt was accented with a sober tie but no jacket. Amber hair still damp from a shower was neatly combed and the black shoes polished to a rich gloss. He looked every inch the quietly successful professional, and she still would have known there was a hidden side to him even if she'd never met him until now.

"Why the secret little smile?" he demanded easily, ushering her into the car before turning to lift a casual hand in greeting to Dara's inquisitive elderly neighbor. Mrs. Jenkins dropped her curtains at once.

"I wish you wouldn't do that," Dara muttered feelingly as Yale slid in beside her.

"It's the highlight of her day. I always wave."

"Oh, Lord!"

"Relax! At your age, what can they say?" he offered cheerfully.

"The same thing neighbors always say in such situations, regardless of the ages of the people involved. And I'm not exactly ancient!" she tacked on, ruffled.

"Of course you aren't, honey," he soothed. "You're exactly the right age."

"For what?" she retorted challengingly.

He ignored that, his hand going to the gearshift with practiced ease as they pulled away from the curb. "You didn't answer my question."

"The smile? I was just thinking how much more relaxing a date is with the gentleman than the . . . other Yale."

"Relaxed, are you? Good. I shall endeavor to be the perfect host," he responded, eyes warm with promise as he slanted her a speculative glance.

And he was. It was predictable, perhaps, that he'd prepared steaks, baked potatoes and a salad, given his culinary taste, but Dara loved every mouthful. His repertoire might be limited, but he did it to perfection.

"I enjoyed that ride today," he said reflectively some time later as he settled her into the deep, dark leather cushions of the couch and sat down beside her. "We must do it again, and soon. How about helping me pick out a bike next weekend? I can't keep sponging off the paperboy."

"It's a deal," she returned, resting her head against his shoulder as he put an arm around her and stretched out his legs with an air of replete satisfaction.

Two snifters of brandy sat on the low table in front of them, a selection of Mozart *Divertimenti* flowed from the expensive stereo and Yale had casually loosened his tie. He looked contented, possibly a bit sleepy and totally unmenacing. Quite the opposite of his alter ego, Dara thought with a hidden chuckle.

"Did you think about what we discussed at lunch, honey?" he asked after a moment, his eyes closed behind his glasses as he leaned his head against the sofa. The fingers of his hand were making absent, lazy movements on her bare arm.

"Yes," she admitted, curling her legs under her pleated skirt and giving herself up to the enjoyment of his warm, unthreatening embrace. "I thought about it."

"And?" he prompted almost neutrally.

"And what?" she murmured, eyes half shut as she burrowed into his shoulder.

"And how long do you think it will take before you're sure of us?"

"You can't put a time limit on things like this, Yale," she protested gently. "There are too many unknowns. Too many variables. Matters simply have to take their course."

"I see," he said quietly after a moment. "You won't even give me a clue?"

How can I, she thought despairingly, when everything hinges on you?

"I'm not going to let myself be rushed into an affair, Yale," she finally said in a soft, firm little voice. "I'm going to be sure, and I want you to be sure."

"I am sure."

"No," she contradicted huskily. "You can't be. Not yet. You may be sure you want to sleep with me, but that's all."

He said nothing for a moment and then he leaned forward and deliberately set his glasses on the table beside the brandy snifters. He settled back into the couch, turning her slightly in his arms and lifting her chin

175

with his free hand. The hazel eyes glittered down into her gray-green ones, and Dara had the first prickles of warning.

"You are a stubborn little thing," he mused, searching her face and lowering his head with lazy intent.

"Everyone's allowed one virtue," she teased, the warning twinges dying out as his mouth covered hers with warmth and masculine longing.

She sighed, twining her arms around his neck. This was the Yale she could handle. The one who would make passionate but gentlemanly love to her and then take her home when she insisted.

"You know this side of me very well now, don't you?" he whispered thickly, his fingers threading through the deep, lustrous red of her hair. Before Dara could answer he had fastened his lips on hers again, moving to deepen the kiss with his tongue.

She felt the gentle probing at her lips and parted them for him with a blissful little moan. After a week of his lovemaking, Dara knew exactly when to call a halt. But the time wasn't yet. For now she could indulge herself.

Her hands moved over his back, investigating the sleek musculature with hunger and the growing passion he elicited so easily. Someday, perhaps soon, he would once again be all hers. But for the moment she would take what she could, that which was safe. . . .

"Dara!"

Her name was a hoarse groan deep in his chest as his fingers found the rising thrust of her breasts.

"I want you," he grated softly, finding her nipples and stroking them through the wispy softness of the dress and lacy bra. "You know that, don't you?"

"Yes, oh, yes, Yale," she breathed, arching into his hands and shivering with pleasure as he lowered the zipper.

It seemed to her that things were moving faster tonight than they usually did. All too soon she would be forced to gently break them off again. She wanted him to slow down so that the end needn't come too quickly. She didn't want to go home to a lonely bed. Not yet.

She closed her eyes as the bodice of the dress was lowered and then drew in her breath as the snap of the lacy bra was freed.

"I love the feel of you," Yale muttered achingly as he cupped her breasts and lowered his head to kiss the rising mounds in his hands. "Full and womanly and so very, very soft. . . ."

"Yale," she began shakily as she was pushed gently backward beneath the weight of his slowly descending body. "Yale, it's getting late. I should be going home."

"Not yet, sweetheart. Not quite yet."

The vague sense of warning rippled to life along her nerve endings. There was a hardness in his words that was unfamiliar. A hardness which belonged to the other Yale.

He stretched out on top of her, his mouth beginning to rain hot, possessive little kisses across her breasts and the smooth skin beneath them, then up along her shoulders. She gasped as his teeth occasionally nipped at her sensitized flesh and her fingers dug into the muscles of his neck and back.

"Tell me you want me," he urged on a groan. "At least give me that much!"

"You know I want you."

"You've wanted me from the first, haven't you? Just as I wanted you!"

"Yale, I think we'd better call a halt," Dara moaned, supremely aware of the weight of his lower body as he thrust it against her in a surging, intimate movement.

"Dara, my darling Dara, I have a confession to make," he drawled slowly, meaningfully.

"What . . . what are you talking about?" she whispered, opening her eyes wide to stare up at him.

His hands locked firmly around her shoulders as if to

hold her still. But she was incapable of movement anyhow. The weight of his body covered her softness with undeniable authority.

The hazel eyes glittered and the lines around his mouth tightened.

"I tricked you," he said intently. "You're not here with your Southern gentleman tonight. You're here with the other Yale. The one who makes you so wary. The one you found when you opened Pandora's box."

"Stop it, Yale! Don't tease me!" she hissed, her fingers clenching into his shoulders.

"I'm not teasing you. The time for that is past. And what's more, I'm not going to let you tease me any longer, either. I'm going to make love to you tonight, sweetheart, the way I did last weekend. I can't wait any longer. Not when you refuse to give me some sort of time limit!"

"Time limit! You want me to put a date on it? Tell you I'll sleep with you on a certain day? That's ridiculous! You know that!"

"This afternoon you were talking months. Honey, I can't wait that long for you! Don't you understand? This past week has been hell, and this afternoon when you started talking about endless weeks ahead I knew I had to do something."

"There's nothing you can do! I've made up my mind, Yale," she retorted gamely, a breathless feeling washing through her. He was serious!

"And I've made up mine," he flung back, a dangerous smile playing about the edges of his hard mouth. "Tonight both hunters are going to close in on you at the same time. I don't think you can resist them both at once!"

Appalled and feeling more helpless than she ever had in her life, Dara knew he was right. His heaviness beat on her senses, mastering her body in a way it seemed to crave.

Without further argument, Yale cut off her moan of protest, sealing her mouth with a kiss that first punished and then soothed. His legs sprawled across hers, anchoring them against the cushions, and Dara felt his hands moving on her body, stripping her clothing from her in long, sweeping gestures.

"Undress me," he ordered gratingly, his lips buried in the hollow of her shoulder. "Touch me with your sweet, loving hands. Touch me, Dara!"

"Please, Yale! This isn't what I want . . . !"

"It will be," he swore. "I'll make it what you want!"

His passion rolled across her like a wave. Soon she lay naked and trembling beneath him. When she refused to undress him, he ripped impatiently at the buttons of his shirt and flung it aside, coming back on top of her at once.

"I've wanted you so badly this week, Dara. I've ached for you. Every time you sent me away I wanted to ignore you. I wanted to tear off your clothes, pull you down on the floor and make love to you until you were no longer capable of speaking the words that would send me away!"

The feel of him was eating into her bones. Dara's senses swam as he talked to her of his need and desire. The passionate phrases were accompanied by an unrelenting assault on her body. His hands explored, caressed and enveloped until her breath came in quick panting gasps.

Through it all she realized dimly that he wasn't even aware of his strongest weapon. He couldn't know how her own sense of rightness was hammering at her, urging her to surrender to the power of the moment. How could a woman deny her man when his need of her was so obvious and so great?

It was impossible. She knew it was going to be impossible long before the first trembling, shuddering response seeped through her defenses.

He was aware of it immediately. When her hands began to slide lovingly over the skin of his back and down to the narrow waist he groaned in satisfaction.

"I knew it," he grated fiercely.

In exultation he strung kisses down her arms to the vulnerable, exquisitely sensitive areas of her elbows and wrists. His hands locked under her buttocks, reveling in the feel of her as he transferred his lips to her curving stomach.

Restlessly, Dara shifted her legs, hugging him between them with feminine strength that served to excite him all the more. Her nails danced on his neck and shoulders as she felt his tongue probing every square inch of her thigh and the soft warm heart of her.

"Oh, Yale, I do want you so . . ." The words were a ribbon of desire that wafted toward him on the wind of passion. He seized the end at once and tugged, drawing her closer and closer.

"Thank God," he cried softly. "Because I couldn't let you go. Not tonight. Not ever. I told you that you were mine!"

"Yes." It was the truth. It had been from the first moment. How could she fight it?

Abruptly he was moving, raising himself from the couch. Before she could ask him why, he reached down and lifted her high into his arms. She closed her eyes again, her hair falling across his shoulder as he carried her wordlessly into the bedroom.

She was gently deposited on the dark down quilt and a moment later, as he shed the last of his clothes and joined her on the bed, Dara knew beyond any doubt that both Yales were united tonight. He was right. She couldn't fight them both, and she no longer wanted to try.

Her arms opened to receive him and he moved against her soft, full curves, crooning like a man in a desert who has found an oasis. The tension between them mounted steadily to dizzying heights as Dara abandoned all attempt at defense. The need to satisfy this most important man in her life was too strong to deny any longer. She would worry about the morning when it came.

"I've dreamed about this every night for the past week. The way you open yourself to me, gather me into you. The silk of your thighs, the responsiveness in you when I touch you like this . . ."

She moaned involuntarily as he claimed the intimate core of her with fingers that sent electricity flying along her veins.

He curled a tongue around one taut nipple and then bit gently, delighting in her reaction.

"Please, Yale. Please . . ." The muttered plea came from the heart of her as she pulled him close.

He obeyed the timeless feminine summons. In the darkness she saw him rise, knew he was going to complete the union and thrilled to the anticipation and need in herself.

And then, like a shattering mirror, everything seemed to fall apart.

"No!"

The cry was torn hoarsely from him as Yale suddenly threw himself to the side, his arm across his eyes in a gesture of abject denial.

"I won't, damn it! I won't do it this way!"

"Yale, what's wrong? What are you saying?"

Trembling, Dara turned her head to look at his rigid length, her eyes full of incomprehension and the still-flaming warmth of the passion he had aroused.

"Get dressed, Dara. For God's sake, get out of here and get dressed!" he rapped bleakly.

Slowly, confusion and fear driving her, Dara sat up beside him. He still refused to uncover his eyes and she could see the tautness in every muscle of his body.

"Yale, I don't understand. . . ."

"Don't be a fool! I'm going to take you home. Exactly as you wanted me to do."

"Why?" The single word was stark and hollow-sounding.

"Because I don't feel like waking up beside you again and going through what I went through last weekend!"

"I . . . I see," she whispered, finally comprehending. Pain washed through her, replacing the love and longing in one fell swoop. She shut her eyes against incipient tears.

"No," he shot back harshly. "I don't think you do."

"Yes, I do," she breathed sadly. "You're afraid that I'll demand another price for the evening and that this time I won't let you escape payment. In the heat of passion you'll offer to pay it, but you suddenly realize that you may not get off the hook tomorrow morning as easily as you did last weekend."

"What the hell . . . !" he began angrily.

"Yale, what if I told you that this time there won't be any price?"

"I'd beat you. With a horsewhip, I think."

"Yale!"

He removed his arm from his eyes and even in the darkness she could see the fire burning in the hazel depths.

"I've had it with you backing out of our arrangements," he snapped, the fury in him unmistakable. "Do you understand? I've had it! You'll let me make love to you and then, in the morning, withdraw yourself from me again. I can't go through that."

"Will you listen to me?" she interrupted, a wild hope warming the cold which had settled on her when he'd broken off the lovemaking.

"No, you'll listen to me! We'll do this your way, Dara, because there doesn't seem to be any alternative, but so help me, when it's finally over I'm going to make you so thoroughly mine that you won't ever again think of that other man. The one with whom everything seemed to click for you!"

"Yale, there is no other man!"

"I know you got rid of him because I made you do it. I don't know why you couldn't overcome the 'complications' in that relationship. You certainly seem strong-willed enough where I'm concerned. But I'll have to be grateful for small favors, I suppose. But eventually you won't ever think of him. What we have between us will be right. You'll hear that magic click, Dara, if you'll listen. I'll make everything right, you'll see!"

"What an idiot you are, Yale Ransom," Dara whispered with deep love. "You were the other man. Everything clicked into place for me the night of the party. Why on earth do you think I left with you after only having known you a couple of hours? Why do you think I pushed so hard to discover the real you? And why do you think I let you make love to me in that sleazy motel room?"

"Dara!"

He sat up beside her, reaching out to grasp her arms and hold her still for his searching gaze. "Dara, are you telling me the truth?"

"I love you, Yale. I have from the first."

"Then why the hell have you put both of us through this?" he demanded violently, giving her a small shake. But she could feel the dawning wonder in him and smiled tremulously.

"Because I wanted you to fall in love with me. Is that so hard to understand? The time I was trying to buy was for you, Yale, not me."

He swore softly, bluntly, and then he pulled her close.

"Dara, you're the idiot. I think I fell in love with you when you gave me your hand to shake so politely at that party and then had the nerve to laugh at me! I knew it for certain the next morning when you woke up in my arms. . . ."

"No," she objected, her face pressed against the tantalizing hair of his chest. "The next morning you talked of fulfilling our arrangement. You were trading your stock account for a night in bed!"

"Sweetheart, it never occurred to me then that you might have fallen in love! The stock account seemed like a perfectly logical way to tie us together. There's nothing like a business arrangement to bring two people into constant contact. And then, the next night when you demanded marriage, I thought I had it made!"

"Only to wake up the next morning and have me tell you that you were free?"

He growled a response, his hands tightening around her. "How could you say that if you love me?"

"I was so crushed that morning when I handed you back your freedom and you took it." Dara sighed. "I thought that if you really cared you would insist on the marriage. Instead you just said okay and walked off into the shower. I could have killed you!"

"I felt the same way about you! I thought you had told me the truth when you claimed to have used the marriage demand only as a means of trying to stop me from making love. When you withdrew the demand, I figured it was because it hadn't worked. The next thing I knew, you were kicking me out of the house!"

"I fed you breakfast first!"

"Lucky me," he drawled, responding unwillingly to her small resurgence of humor. "I decided then and there that you were going to find out exactly what you'd done when you'd pushed past my carefully concocted image. As far as I was concerned, you had uncovered the truth and you were stuck with it!"

"I've always believed in being responsible for one's

own actions," she teased warmly, trailing her fingers lovingly along the muscle of his arm.

"I almost flipped when you started talking about this mysterious other man," he grated. "The one with whom you claimed everything had 'clicked.'"

"I know." She smiled shakily, remembering his threatening lovemaking.

"Sweetheart, was it really me? The one you were so sure about?"

"I was sure about my feelings for you. I wasn't at all sure about yours for me! That was the complication I spoke of."

She felt the thankful sigh as he exhaled and held her more tightly than ever. "No other woman has ever been interested in knowing all of me," he said softly. "No one has ever guessed there was more than what showed on the surface. You took one look at me and started pressing for all the answers. I was stunned. By the time I had you in bed at that motel I knew I was going to have to make you mine. I couldn't let you go. You knew too much about me!"

"Well, I wasn't prepared for the split personality!"

"I was desperate and determined," he confided. "I had to find some way of throwing you off balance. You were so controlled, so cool about it all. I told myself I'd wear you down with a two-pronged attack."

"The old hunting knowledge from the hills?" She smiled, inhaling the musky scent of him.

"I was prepared to keep it up for quite a while, but today, when you started talking in terms of months, I decided I'd had it!"

"So tonight I was dating the devil in disguise?"

"Umm. Let's just say you had the whole me."

"An unnerving thought."

"You can handle it," he promised, pulling aside the dark sweep of her hair and pressing a hungry kiss to the back of her neck.

"This time you really will have to marry me, Yale," she vowed, sliding her hands down to his hips and sinking her nails ever so gently into him.

"Oh, no, you don't. I'm not taking any chances on your proposals. I will do the proposing this time. And you can bet your sweet life I won't renege like some folks do! Will you marry me, Dara? I warn you that if you say no, it won't make any difference. You're going to come and live with me regardless of your answer!"

"What can I say? You've closed all the avenues of escape! I'll marry you." She pulled her head back for a moment and smiled up at him dreamily. "I wouldn't want your reputation to suffer. Not after you've spent so many years building it!"

"I love you, Dara," he growled softly, the humor in him fading before the force of renewed passion.

"I love you, my gentleman devil. I always will."

He pushed her back into the thickness of the quilt, his hands running over her with a new possessiveness from ankle to thigh.

She felt the sudden urgency in him and knew it was echoed in herself. For both of them the need to consummate the private vows they had just taken was fierce and strong. The slow, leisurely lovemaking would come later, Dara knew. Now the urgency of committing themselves to each other was too great to allow for the languid, luxurious kind of love.

Within moments, Yale had restoked her level of excitement to what it had been before he had broken off so abruptly. She knew he felt the heat in her and the welcoming between her thighs.

With a groan of need and aching desire he covered her, surrendering to her femininity even as she surrendered to the bold, uncompromising maleness in him.

"Dara, my darling Dara," he husked, uniting with her in thrilling mastery.

She sang his name into his throat as he closed with her and pulled her into the surging rhythm of his body. Deliriously she gave herself up to the joy of the lovemaking, knowing even as she did so that he was demanding everything of her this time.

Together they sought the heights of the mountains above the verdant valley and together they sailed off into the currents of air that wafted them gently to the green fields below.

Dara was aware of the strength of Yale's hold and knew she was clinging just as tightly to him. This time neither would let go. Ever. This time everything really was right. It all clicked.

Much later, Dara roused sufficiently from the comforting power of Yale's arms to smile lovingly down into his relaxed features.

"And why are you sitting up there, looking like the cat that got the canary?" He grinned, ruffling her hair with deep love.

"I was just thinking," she murmured on a thread of laughter, "that when the chips were down tonight, the Southern gentleman resurfaced at the last moment."

He grinned back lazily, the gold in his teeth taunting her. "You think so?"

"Of course," she mocked. "Why else would you have stopped at such a crucial point earlier?"

"I've told you before, I'm a very good hunter," he drawled.

She blinked uncertainly. "Are you telling me you planned that?"

"Now that you've reunited both sides of my personality, you're going to have that problem a lot, I'm afraid," he told her with patently false sympathy.

"What problem?"

"Not knowing for sure which Yale you're dealing with."

"Hah! I know you, Yale Ransom," she declared with serene confidence. "You won't be able to fool me that easily!"

"Whatever you say, ma'am," he agreed politely.

Dara leaned down to kiss the Southern gentleman and surrendered in delight to the devil who reached out to pull her into his arms.

Silhouette Desire 15-Day Trial Offer

A new romance series that explores contemporary relationships in exciting detail

Six Silhouette Desire romances, free for 15 days! We'll send you six new Silhouette Desire romances to look over for 15 days, absolutely free! If you decide not to keep the books, return them and owe nothing.

Six books a month, free home delivery. If you like Silhouette Desire romances as much as we think you will, keep them and return your payment with the invoice. Then we will send you six new books every month to preview, just as soon as they are published. You pay only for the books you decide to keep, and you never pay postage and handling.

Silhouette Desire

Coming Next Month

Price of Surrender by Stephanie James

Holt Sinclair thought everything had its price until he met a woman who couldn't be bought. Adena West had come to him on business but Holt was more interested in pleasure. She entered his corporate jungle to become passion's prey.

Sweet Serenity by Billie Douglass

When Serena was a child, Tom Reynolds destroyed her happy life. With Tom's reappearance all the old hurt returned. Although he made her tremble with passion, Serena vowed not to fall beneath his spell.

Gentle Conquest by Kathryn Mallory

When rock star Stuart North agreed to buy and preserve historic Brogan House, he wanted gray-eyed Robin Elliot as part of the deal. What he didn't bargain for was the electricity between them that burst into a flashfire of passion.

Silhouette Desire

Coming Next Month

Seduction by Design by Erin St. Claire

From the very beginning Tyler Scott made his intentions clear to Hailey — he intended to be her lover. He radiated a raw masculine power that left Hailey helpless with desire and unable to resist him.

Shadow of Betrayal by Nicole Monet

Diana Moreland tried to hate Joshua Cambridge especially now that he returned to claim his son; the nephew she raised all alone. Desperately she fought to keep the child and her heart — and lost both.

Ask Me No Secrets by Ruth Stewart

The past was behind her, and when Allison looked into Forrest Bennett's coal-black eyes she knew the future held a glowing promise of love. But would he love her still when he penetrated to the secret heart of her passion?

YOU'LL BE SWEPT AWAY
WITH SILHOUETTE DESIRE

$1.75 each

1 ☐ CORPORATE AFFAIR
James

2 ☐ LOVE'S SILVER WEB
Monet

3 ☐ WISE FOLLY
Clay

4 ☐ KISS AND TELL Carey

5 ☐ WHEN LAST WE LOVED
Baker

6 ☐ A FRENCHMAN'S KISS
Mallory

7 ☐ NOT EVEN FOR LOVE
Claire

8 ☐ MAKE NO PROMISES
Dee

9 ☐ MOMENT IN TIME
Simms

10 ☐ WHENEVER I LOVE YOU
Smith

$1.95 each

11 ☐ VELVET TOUCH
James

12 ☐ THE COWBOY AND THE
LADY Palmer

13 ☐ COME BACK, MY LOVE
Wallace

14 ☐ BLANKET OF STARS
Valley

15 ☐ SWEET BONDAGE
Vernon

16 ☐ DREAM COME TRUE
Major

17 ☐ OF PASSION BORN
Simms

18 ☐ SECOND HARVEST
Ross

19 ☐ LOVER IN PURSUIT
James

20 ☐ KING OF DIAMONDS
Allison

21 ☐ LOVE IN THE CHINA SEA
Baker

22 ☐ BITTERSWEET IN BERN
Durant

23 ☐ CONSTANT STRANGER
Sunshine

24 ☐ SHARED MOMENTS
Baxter

25 ☐ RENAISSANCE MAN
James

26 ☐ SEPTEMBER MORNING
Palmer

27 ☐ ON WINGS OF NIGHT
Conrad

28 ☐ PASSIONATE JOURNEY
Lovan

29 ☐ ENCHANTED DESERT
Michelle

30 ☐ PAST FORGETTING
Lind

31 ☐ RECKLESS PASSION
James

32 ☐ YESTERDAY'S DREAMS
Clay

33 ☐ PROMISE ME
TOMORROW Powers

34 ☐ SNOW SPIRIT
Milan

35 ☐ MEANT TO BE
Major

36 ☐ FIRES OF MEMORY
Summers

SILHOUETTE DESIRE, Department SD/6
1230 Avenue of the Americas
New York, NY 10020

Please send me the books I have checked above. I am enclosing $_____
(please add 50¢ to cover postage and handling. NYS and NYC residents please add
appropriate sales tax.) Send check or money order—no cash or C.O.D's please.
Allow six weeks for delivery.

NAME _____

ADDRESS _____

CITY _____ STATE/ZIP _____